I0599399

SILENT CITY

MIKE BENNETT

RYAN
PUBLISHING

First published 2022 by Ryan Publishing
PO Box 7680, Melbourne, 3004
Victoria, Australia
Ph: 61 3 9505 6820
Email: books@ryanpub.com
Website: www.ryanpub.com

RYAN
PUBLISHING

 A catalogue record for this
book is available from the
National Library of Australia

Title: *Silent City – Make Your Own Luck*
Paperback: 9781876498948
eBook: 9781876498955

Internal and cover design by Luke Harris, Working Type Studio, Victoria, Australia. www.workingtype.com.au
Edited by Graeme Ryan

CONTENTS

In loving memory of my best friend,
David Michael Gray, casino operator extraordinaire.
Enigmatic, engaging, selfless, supportive.
Sorely missed.

ACKNOWLEDGEMENTS

With two pre-school kids and working from home in the first years of the Covid pandemic, my daughter-in-law Jess Bennett burned the midnight oil while editing my struggling attempts at writing this novel. Words are unable to thank her enough for her commitment, attention to detail, and female insights which have shaped and bettered this work.

From the inception of *Silent City* my Italian friend Luca Morsella called upon his vast experience as a film director and producer to both encourage and inspire me to write the story as 'visually' as possible — as if the reader were watching a movie.

Tragically Luca passed away before his time and never read the completed *Silent City*. I hope you would have enjoyed it, il mio amico, il mio mentore.

I need to thank my close friend of some 50 years, Peter Julian Bible, for allowing me to steal his identity and to use an actual life-experience of his in the narrative.

Marg Rothenburg needs a big hug and appreciation for her initial artwork which inspired the final book cover illustration.

Others along the way to whom I owe a debt of gratitude for their continued encouragement to press on with the book include Nadya Vella, Alexe Von Brockdorf, Derek Jones, John and Marlene Rickus, Maria English and my son, Tom Bennett.

Finally, thank you Graeme Ryan and Luke Harris for the hand-holds, sage advice, and guidance in bringing this work from manuscript to publication.

CHAPTER ONE

ATLANTIC CITY - OCEANIC RESORT

An impatient beep on his pager interrupted Douglas Browning as he sipped a cappuccino in the Neptune Lounge. Being almost in the centre of the casino, the elevated lounge provided a good vantage point. From there he could see most of the action in the table games section of the casino, just a few metres away. The remainder of the gaming hall was filled by line upon line of slot machines, punctuated by smaller groups of three and four here, circles of ten there.

Each machine had been positioned to maximise traffic flow and increase play. Every line, group or bank of machines had its own audio signature — bells, chimes, pay-line music, excited raised voices of winners and the shouted disbelief of losers — a cacophony that never stopped.

On a dais in the centre of the lounge a petit redhead was playing a grand piano, giving it all she had and singing her heart out to a small, disinterested gathering. Winners, losers, lovers and working girls thought Browning, the usual sort of crowd. He saw the redhead smile at him, so he smiled back, unsure if the smile was really meant for him or simply an entertainer's smile, part of the show.

He turned his attention back to the casino floor. Although not the biggest in town, the casino in the Oceanic Resort had sixty plus table games and around two thousand slot machines, a sizeable operation just the same. From his vantage point, leaning on the counter of the lounge's bar, he could see along the rows of blackjack tables. They were thinly populated, not much happening there.

A pit boss was engaged in an animated conversation with a cocktail waitress, her empty tray parked on her hip as he waggled his forefinger at her. He caught Browning's stare and immediately shooed her away, busying himself over the computer on a desk in the middle of the pit, his head down to avoid further eye contact with Browning.

Browning sighed and turned his attention to the roulette tables across to his right, all of which were fairly busy. Behind them three craps tables struggled for a game, judging by the indifferent calling of the action by the stickmen. He could hear their calls, but only just. When they had a decent game going, they could be heard then alright, no problem. Banging their sticks loudly they swirled the dice around the tables, cajoling players to bet, calling the result of the latest throw of the dice. "Seven out – lines in – don'ts win"

He unclipped the pager from his belt and read 'Code 2' on the message display — call surveillance. He turned and motioned the barman to pass the phone from under the counter. He lifted the handset and had to cover his other ear with his free hand to block out the sudden fanfare of jackpot trumpets from a nearby slot machine. The squeals of an excited middle-aged woman were louder than the trumpets. She jumped up and down, waving her hands in the air. "I've won, I've won," she screamed, over and over. He smiled at her antics as he spoke into the phone.

¶

"Douglas here, watcha got Paulie?" Paul Giacono was Head of Surveillance at the Oceanic. Browning liked him. They'd struck up a good relationship in the three years since Browning arrived.

"You better come up here and take a look, I'm a thinking," said Paulie in his New York Queens accent, "a working crew we have in tonight." Browning frowned. "On my way," he said. The crew Paulie referred to would be a team of professional cheats — the last thing he expected to find mid-shift on a quiet night.

He turned to face the barman and pushed the phone back to him. "Who's the girl?" he asked, nodding towards the redhead. She was singing a Billy Joel number. Browning thought she sounded slightly out of key. He winced as she missed a note, hoping she hadn't noticed.

"New act that one," said the Barman, "just started tonight – ain't she great?"

Browning smiled at him. "Well, she's pretty enough. Might be good if she could sing though, don't you think? What's her name?"

"Nina Meadows."

Browning was taken aback. "Nina Meadows, as in Philip Meadows?"

"The very same. Niece I think," said the Barman, rolling his eyes.

Browning considered this news. Philip Meadows was a high profile, charismatic entrepreneur. One of his companies had recently acquired a majority shareholding in the Oceanic, amidst much hype in the Atlantic City media.

And now his niece was appearing at the Oceanic. Interesting.

"Well, now you mention it, I guess she does have a certain style," he said with a grin. The barman shrugged his shoulders and grinned back. "If you say so. You the boss."

Browning spooned up the froth on his cappuccino. As he left, he took a last quick look at Nina Meadows, hoping for another smile.

CHAPTER TWO

OCEANIC - SURVEILLANCE

A t the door to the surveillance room Browning entered his personal code into a wall mounted keypad and let himself in. He stood still for a moment, waiting for his vision to adjust to the level of light in the room, which was lit by the glowing screens of eighty TV monitors of varying sizes. There were large areas of shadow, and he knew from painful experience how easy it was to bump into something before your eyes adjusted. The room was quiet except for the background hum of the air conditioning and heat exchange units necessary to maintain the correct temperature to cope with the power output of some two hundred VCR units, one for each camera in the casino. Banks of switcher units and computers managed all camera activity as directed by the surveillance team, recording everything as it happened on the casino floor.

The brightest light came from the central monitor on the nearest console. Around this big screen were eight smaller screens and underneath this array were another dozen small screens, six upon six, at the level of the console desktop. The smaller screens were show-ing various sensitive points around the facility including emergency exits, the main casino entrance lobby, the lines of slot machines and an exterior view of the cashier's cage. With a time interval of one frame every two seconds, these monitors provided a continual 24-hour view of the activity in those areas. But the delay between frames made the action look jumpy, unreal almost. A trained surveil-lance operator only saw these smaller screens out of the corner of the eye but instinctively knew when their coverage warranted a closer look. The operator would then view the area in question with a PTZ camera — Pan, Tilt and Zoom — and new, real-time images would be put up on one of the bigger screens on the main array which were otherwise used to show images of table games or slot machine play, automatically switching the coverage. Surveillance also monitored player behaviour and sometimes an operator would track various persons as they circulated the casino floor.

There were four of these consoles in the surveillance room, all configured with the same array of monitors. During peak hours or on a busy weekend they would all be manned. At such times Paulie would patrol the room, moving back and forth behind each operator's chair, adding his instincts and experienced eyes to theirs.

Browning's eyes slowly accustomed and he could see Paulie sitting back in an operator's chair at console number one, looking up at the main screen. He turned to Browning. "Hey Doug, how 'ya doing?" while rolling an unlit cigar stub around his lips.

"Okay I guess – and you?"

"Well, I'm good now, I was totally bored earlier. But things are looking up, I'm a-thinking! Take a look at this crew." Turning back to the console he rolled out a stool from under the desk, motioning

Browning to sit. "I'll show you their mechanic," he said as he maneuvered the joystick on the control panel. The image on the main monitor screen enlarged as he zoomed in the camera, and focused upon a tall, thin, dark haired man playing roulette.

"This guy's the mechanic. He's some artist, very smooth," he said, pointing at the screen with the cigar stub. "He's a little too quick though. That's how I got him." He looked at Browning. "Took a quick look at our bad guy files, but no go. Over at Borgata they got facial recognition, pick him in a second. But we still got pictures in a file. You know him?"

Browning looked intently at the mechanic. He thought he looked Eastern European, the high cheekbones and pale skin. He stood at the bottom of the table, placing chips on lots of numbers. In the few moments that he watched him play, Browning did not see any late bets being placed. He answered Paulie without looking away from the screen. "No. Don't recall seeing him before. Where's the decoy?"

Paulie put the cigar stub back in his mouth. Turning back to the console he rotated the joystick and the camera focused upon a small man sitting a couple of seats away from the mechanic. "That's him?" Browning sounded surprised. "He doesn't look old enough to be in here even!"

Paulie nodded. "Well, he's already pressing up and they ain't been playing all that long, so there might be another one in this crew I'm a thinking," he said.

Browning continued to stare at the baby-faced decoy, he looked about fourteen he thought, so there was a good chance that security had copped his ID when he came in. "Can't say I've seen him before either," he said.

Browning returned his attention to the mechanic. He was

playing using blue coloured chips. There are two kinds of chips for play on an American roulette game. 'Colour chips' are just that, seven or eight sets of different colours on each table with a distinctive design for each table, a butterfly, a triangle, etc. This ensures that each player can identify his own chips and winning bets. When a player wants to stop playing on a particular table then the colour chips are exchanged for 'cash chips' which have values stamped on them and which are negotiable in the casino. Players can then exchange them for cash at the cash desk. In some casinos they can buy drinks with them over the bar, and cocktail waitresses can accept them for tips and cash them out at the cash desk.

Typically, a mechanic played with colour chips and placed two or three at a time on several numbers each time the ball was spun. When the 'hit' was on, the mechanic would place three chips on the winning number after the ball dropped, the bottom one being a cash chip, the other two being his colour chips. This is known as 'top hatting'.

Most times the table inspector or the dealer would see this as a late bet and the dealer would remove the mechanic's colour chips but the cash chip he placed would remain on the winning number. Then the mechanic's partner, the decoy, would claim the winnings for the cash chip.

When the move was not noticed, both the mechanic and the decoy collected the payout from the winning number.

Some crews used a runner, to whom the decoy would surreptitiously pass high value chips for cashing out at the cage. Teams of pickpockets use the same move when moving a stolen item from the dip (the actual thief) to a second or even third member of the team. This left the dip clean if he was apprehended. So, the passing of chips to a runner would enable the mechanic and decoy to continue working the table without piling up lots of cash chips and drawing undue attention to themselves. The decoy would regularly ask the dealer for bigger chips, changing twenty-fives for hundreds.

Typically, only one-hundred-dollar chips would be passed to a runner to cash out because someone asking to cash out five-hundred-dollar chips at the cage would require the cashier to ask which table they came from. The cashier would then check with the pit boss to see if a player had indeed left the table with any five-hundred-dollar chips.

This was the last thing a runner wanted, as a runner never played. When a crew finished playing at the table the decoy could cash out the five-hundred-dollar chips without problem as the cashier's inquiry with the pit boss would be confirmed.

So, when the decoy started pressing up early on, it made Paulie think this crew had a runner. Otherwise, the decoy would simply continue playing without 'pressing up' by exchanging smaller denomination chips for bigger ones until they were ready to leave.

He turned to look at Paulie. "You think there's a runner as well? Baby Face here setting up for a pass?" "Yeah, I think so, that's why I called you up here. I had a good look at the tapes and found these two coming in, ten minutes apart. Baby Face was first in the casino but not first to the table. The mechanic was already playing when he took a seat."

He paused as something on a delayed time-frame monitor caught his eye and he quickly put a real time image of the staff entry door onto the main monitor. After a moment or two he grunted and changed the view back to Roulette 3. "I don't wanna pick 'em up and call the cops until we have 'em all in the frame, assuming there is a runner," he said, rubbing his eyes with both fists. He looked at Browning. "Your call Doug, you wanna hang on and see if there's a runner or pull 'em in? Either way they're gonna stop real soon I'm a thinking. Don't know why exactly, just a feeling I have."

"If they're going to stop so soon, why do they need a runner, Paulie?"

"Don't know. Who knows what these people think?" He took the cigar stub out of his mouth and pointed it at Browning as he spoke. "Maybe this is a rehearsal. First time out together. Anyway, your call."

Browning looked back to the monitor as he considered the situation. In order for the casino to detain anyone there had to be evidence of wrong doing on tape and this needed to be verified by the Operations Shift Manager and a surveillance operator before the New Jersey State Police were called in to make an arrest. With a roulette crew, a tape of the mechanic 'top-hatting' by placing late bets did not always, in itself, constitute enough worthwhile evidence to satisfy the police that a charge would stick in court. This depended a lot on the view of the individual officers who arrived in response to the call and the quality of the surveillance tape, showing the mechanic at work.

To be sure of satisfying the police, another tape of the decoy and/or a runner cashing out chips was also needed as this act constituted the actual crime of accepting monies in exchange for chips that were fraudulently acquired. It was rare for the police not to arrest in instances when this corroborating tape was shown.

When surveillance identified and filmed a crew at work, they would tell the Operations Shift Manager who would then instruct security to detain them in a room just off the casino floor, until the police arrived. That's how it worked in Atlantic City. Browning had worked in less high-profile places in other countries where the casino management would not bother calling the police. They would simply take some big guys and a baseball bat into the room with them. All the better to explain the situation to the hapless crew.

"Paulie, the tape's good? Several hits?" Browning asked, referring to the number of times the mechanic had struck. "Yeah, you bet. You wanna see it now?" He turned to a bank of VCR machines stacked, floor to ceiling, in a rack to his right.

"No, you tell me it's kosher then that's okay, I'll see it later. Right now, I better go down, nose around, see if I can spot the runner in case they do stop soon. Trusting your instincts on this one."

Paulie nodded, "Okey Dokey! I'll work on it from here and get John Long up to speed by the time you hit the floor." Long was the security Shift Manager on duty and his men would make the collar when the time came, detaining the crew until the police arrived.

"Okay, is he in fancy dress tonight?" asked Browning. Paulie nodded and laughed. 'Fancy dress' was how Browning referred to security managers dressed in casual clothes, rather than the customary lounge suit and tie. Now for some reason, Paulie seemed to find this amusing.

Browning looked around the room, only Paulie's console was on full operation, the others all in standby mode. "You on your own tonight?"

"Yeah, until two when my graveyard shift comes on. It was pretty quiet, so I gave Chas an early night." Chas Casapinta was Paulie's number two who had an amazing gift for faces, a 'photographic' memory. Browning was thinking that Chas would probably know the mechanic and Baby Face, they both looked a little unusual.

"Okay I'm off. Let's keep close on this," he said, shadow boxing with a large mushroom-shaped push-button that opened the door, dancing lightly to and fro on his toes. "We may not have much time, so use my cell phone. Don't bother with the pager," and he went, striking the exit button with a straight left jab.

CHAPTER THREE

ESTONIA - TALLINN

The Viceroy Hotel was built in 1900 on the corner of Niguliste and Rataskarvu, quite close to the Niguliste Museum and Concert Hall and not far from the Danish King's Garden. This area, to the west of the centre of Estonia's capital city, Tallinn, had seen better times in the pre-communist era but was now enjoying a gradual revival as investors turned forlorn and dilapidated buildings into modern apartments and offices with all 'mod-cons', whilst retaining and restoring the original façades and imbuing the area with the relaxed look and ambience of a bygone era.

The Viceroy had also been completely renovated yet remained a hotel, with around a hundred and fifty rooms where before there had been a hundred, as economies of scale were brought to bear by the new owners. Although they retained the façade of the Viceroy and a 'Victorian' feel to the public areas, they had changed the ballroom into a casino. In the times when the Viceroy was built no self-respecting hotel could survive without a ballroom, and the Viceroy's had been the number one venue for Tallinn's elite who would arrive in horse-drawn carriages, complete with footmen, to carouse the night away dancing to live orchestras and string quartets. The ballroom's twenty-foot-high French windows along the south wall, through which the freezing coachmen could see their Patrons revelling inside, had been retained so that the hotel façade remained unchanged. Inside the casino the windows had been covered by panels with art-deco wall lights, in a style more reminiscent of the 1920s than of Queen Victoria's time with the walls between the panelled windows covered from floor to ceiling in blue velvet drapes. Three large, tiered crystal chandeliers dominated the centre of the room, their lights dimmed in deference to the traditional shaded lights hanging over each of the gaming tables and to reduce ambient light interference to the CCTV coverage provided by the many cameras housed in black perspex domes, mounted on the ceilings.

The décor in the 'Casino Sinine' was predominantly blue, the drapes, the carpet and the layouts on the blackjack and roulette tables. Perhaps this was how the casino got its name, 'Sinine' meaning blue in Estonian.

For a midweek evening the room was fairly busy, with American roulette proving more popular than blackjack or punto-banco on this particular night. Goodbook and Door were at a roulette table, Cliff Door was the mechanic, one of the very best around, and Julian Goodbook was the decoy with a 'nose' for trouble that rarely let him down. Unusually for a decoy he was a big man who did not easily blend in with the crowd around him, he stood out rather than being inconspicuous. Somehow this worked in his favour, as he was rarely picked out by surveillance or security. They were a formidable combination, a tight crew.

Door was moving smoothly, right in the zone, placing late bets every few spins or so on the winning number and then, when the inspector called "late bet", simply removing his colour chips from the numbered square on the table layout with a charming apology and a silly smile that slightly inebriated people are wont to give. Except he wasn't even remotely tipsy, and the cash value chips he had also placed on the winning number remained, unseen by the dealer or the inspector as having been placed after the ball dropped. Simple! The trick was to be flowing in one's movements around the numbered layout, placing small colour chip bets in a continuous, unhurried manner until the ball dropped and then placing the slug, a couple of colour chips with one or two cash value chips underneath them, on the winning number. A lot depended on where the winning number was in relation to the mechanic's position over the betting area and if the number in question lay empty on the table when the ball dropped. The mechanic has a split second to decide to lay the 'top hat', the slug of chips, or not. Any slight hesitation to lay the bet would alter the flow of the mechanic's movements, causing a slightly quicker motion when laying the slug than the other bets the mechanic had placed. Being too quick could give the game away.

Goodbook sat two seats away, playing mainly small amounts with cash value chips on the even chance bets and collecting the payouts for the cash chips Door had 'top-hatted' onto the winning numbers.

He calculated they were up about ten thousand Kroons, almost nine hundred US dollars, not bad for 20 minutes work, when he saw it. A suited security man standing by the cash desk put his right hand on the left lapel on his jacket and, turning his head a little, mouthed a couple of syllables – his left hand went to his left ear and pressed his radio earpiece as if to make it work better, then he looked up and nodded at a small CCTV camera dome mounted on the ceiling in the centre of the room. Nothing so unusual in that but Goodbook caught the man's second look – directly at Door! It was very slight, but Goodbook saw it. Time to go!

He picked up his cash chips and stood up to move away from the table, knocking his chair into the person seated next to him as he did so. "Strewth," he said, in an unmistakeable Aussie drawl, "sorry mate," and headed off towards the cash desk.

Heeding the coded warning, Door turned to the table inspector and made a sign to him with his hand, as if holding a glass. "Waitress please," he said

The inspector nodded at him with a smile, "sure, no problem" he said, with an accent more Scandinavian than Eastern European, looking around the room for a coffee waitress. Door looked around with him and saw two 'suits' heading his way, very relaxed in their approach he noted, not wishing to alert the target, well trained.

He stood up, stacking his chips neatly on the table as he again signed to the inspector – he pointed at the chips then at himself and the toilet area. Again, the Inspector nodded, he would keep an eye on Door's chips.

As Door moved away from the table, he heard Goodbook's cry, "Bloody Nora," and he glanced back to see him dropping his chips on the floor. In one movement the big man dropped onto one knee and began scrabbling with some urgency to pick them up, knocking into the advancing security men as he did so.

One of them kneeled to assist him, picking up chips, and Goodbook grabbed the arm of the other as if to stop losing his balance, before he stood up again. The kneeling suit stood up and gave him the chips he had collected and Goodbook thanked him profusely, shaking hands with both of them. The suits turned back towards the table where Door was playing, looking concerned and standing on tip toe, stretching their necks, and looking this way and that in an effort to locate him, but he was gone.

CHAPTER FOUR

OCEANIC – CASINO FLOOR

Going down the internal stairwell to the casino floor Browning paused for a moment to call John Long, the Security Manager on shift. Long answered at the first ring. "Hey Doug, on my way to see Paulie now," he said, in his customary Texan drawl.

"Okay good, can you put a uniform by the cage and two by the nearest entrance to Roulette 3?"

"It's in hand already Doug."

"Good man, I'm going there now for a look-see. You're in plain clothes tonight, right?"

"Sure thing pardner," drawled Long, "see you there soon as I check the tape with Paulie."

Browning hung up, removed his ID badge and entered the casino floor. Walking casually towards a bank of slot machines near Roulette 3 he paused at a gap between two banks of 'Triple 7s' slot machines to look over to the cage.

The uniformed security guard he asked for was already there, standing by the counter as if waiting for a 'fill'. One of security's tasks was to carry chips from the cage to gaming tables when their chip banks had run low, in which case the pit boss would call for a fill.

Satisfied the uniform was in position Browning continued along, appearing to look at the pay tables on the row of slots but watching the activity around Roulette 3 in the reflection of the machine's glass panels. He called the control room.

"Yo," said Paulie, "I was just going to call you, Long John is on his way, should be right there." Browning smiled. Everyone called John Long 'Long John', probably on account of him being six feet seven in his socks.

Paulie continued, "The decoy's palming his cash chips, looks like he's gonna make a pass, I'm a thinking!" Browning nodded, pressing the phone to his ear, whilst grinning and making gesticulations with his free hand, as if someone was telling him a joke. "Stay on the line Paulie" he said.

Moving slowly along the bank of slots, still waving his hands around and keeping up the pretence of an animated conversation, he edged closer and closer to Roulette 3, scanning the room as he grinned and smiled into the phone. His eye was taken by a striking blonde woman, strolling along the walkway between the rows of tables. She had the look about her of an up-market working girl but despite showing a lot of leg under a blue, full skirted dress, he knew she was not a hooker. He broke off his mimed conversation and spoke to Paulie, "See the blonde, blue dress, approaching from roulette 2?" There was a pause and Browning could hear the cigar stub being worked around Paulie's mouth.

"Yeah, got her now, this the runner?" "I think so," said Browning, looking intently at the blonde. "This is the pass, it's gonna happen now!"

"Okay," said Paulie, but Browning never heard him, he had already dropped his phone hand down to his side and was again looking intently at the pay tables on the slots, once more using the reflections in the glass panels to keep a close eye on the blonde. Then he saw John Long approaching and almost burst out laughing.

Long was wearing the classic Texan cowboy outfit, tight jeans, boots, oversized jacket, bootlace tie with a cow-skull and, to top it all, a Stetson hat. With the boots and the hat Long looked about eight feet tall. Some plain clothes outfit, at least nobody would pick him for security thought Browning. Long took up station by Roulette 2, looking intently at the electronic number display by the roulette wheel, just another punter.

The blonde was closing in on Roulette 3, drifting along, smiling, not a care in the world, just a slightly tipsy girl out on the town. As common-place and un-remarkable in a casino as Long's cowboy, it occurred to Browning. Well, in America anyway.

Wobbling a little, unsteady on her heels on the lush carpet perhaps, the blonde passed Roulette 3, brushed the decoy lightly as she checked her balance and continued on her way without pausing. She disappeared from Browning's view around the end of the bank of machines where he stood. He raised the phone, "Paulie, was that it? I can't be sure from here."

"Yup, they passed, they're good alright. But I got 'em cold," he said, his voice distorted by the movement of the cigar circling around his mouth. To Browning it sounded like "butty gum gold!" He smiled and looked up at the ceiling. Like most older style US casinos, Oceanic featured mirrored ceiling panels as part of the décor. These were a legacy of a time when surveillance personnel patrolled along catwalks hidden in the void above the false ceiling and looked down through the mirrored panels to monitor activity on the casino floor below. Nowadays, state of the art CCTV proved a better option, replacing live patrols and removing an un-necessary strain on the budget.

Browning watched the blonde in the ceiling mirrors as she sauntered along. "She's heading for the cage Paulie," he said into the cell phone, "you ready?"

"Up for it, I'm a thinking," was Paulie's reply. Browning could hear the excitement in his voice.

"Good man," he said, snapping the phone shut and open again in one movement. He called John Long, "John, they made the pass, blonde girl, blue dress, on her way to cash out. Keep close tabs on the crew."

"Roger that," said Long.

Browning moved towards the cage and looking at Roulette 3 saw that the mechanic was already changing up his colour chips, but the decoy was gone! Long was on his cell phone, presumably talking to his guys to detain the decoy on his way out, at least Browning hoped. Long looked directly at him and touched his Stetson with his forefinger, as if to confirm that everything was under control.

The blonde was taking cash chips from her handbag and stacking them on the counter at the cage as Browning approached. The uniformed security guard that Long had sent over was already in position a few feet behind her, close enough to ensure quick physical contact if needed but not too close to alarm her.

She smiled at the cashier and tapped her stacked chips lightly with her forefinger. In a very soft voice said, "I make that twenty-two hundred exactly," and pushed the stack towards the opening in the cage window. The cashier smiled back at her as he counted the chips, re-arranging them into four stacks of five and two separate chips. He nodded as he confirmed the amount. "Yes M'am, twenty-two one-hundred-dollar chips, two thousand two hundred dollars in total." He moved the chips towards him, through the aperture in the glass and placed them to one side so that the blonde would be unable to reach them, and looked at Browning who was now by her side, leaning in a very relaxed manner on the cage counter

"Excuse me miss," he said, holding out his ID badge towards her with his right hand. "Douglas Browning, Operations Shift Manager," he paused, smiling, "I'd like you to accompany me to our office please."

The blonde looked at him, glancing at the ID badge briefly before she turned to face him square on, swaying slightly as if off balance. "Well now, why would I want to do that?" she said, pausing to take another look at his badge as if to confirm his name. She paused again, placing her handbag on the counter between them, tinkering nervously with the clasp with the fingers of her right hand, "what for?"

"I think you know what for miss," he replied. He touched his right ear lobe with his finger and thumb. The uniform saw the signal and moved up close behind the blonde. Browning continued, "The officer here will show you the way as we have some questions we would like to ask you about these chips and how you acquired them please." His smile remained but his casual stance did not as he moved slightly away from the counter, standing straight.

The security guard took hold of her left arm with his right hand and said, "If you would come along with me now, please miss," and started to guide her away from the counter. She stumbled slightly, off balance, and the guard instinctively turned square on to her to prevent her from falling. She backed away from him, pulling a can of mace from her handbag and aiming it directly at his face. Browning struck her full force on her right ear, his left arm still extended as she stood rigid for a nano-second, the unfired can still in her grasp, before sliding slowly onto the floor with the guard still holding her left arm and now kneeling alongside her.

"Boss you knocked her cold," the guard said looking up at Browning. "I can't believe you did that." Browning kneeled beside him and removed the can of mace from the woman's hand. He showed it to the guard, "This could have blinded you."

The guard took the can and looked back at Browning, who was flexing the fingers of his left hand. "Wow, geez, it all happened so quick I never even saw it." The blonde was trying to sit up, but not finding it easy. Moving around behind her the guard assisted her into a sitting position. He looked nervously at Browning as John Long arrived on the scene. "Boss, you still struck a woman here," he whispered, "I don't know if that's okay, people get the wrong idea about these things."

Browning looked at him, then up at Long and turned back to the blonde. He reached out and put his hand on her hair and tugged at it. The wig came off easily enough, revealing dark hair, crew cut in military style. He handed the blonde's wig up to Long then leaned over and lightly tapped the blonde under her chin with his fingers. "How are you Pierre, you feeling okay now?" he said, still smiling.

The blonde looked up at him and said, in a deep masculine voice, "Go fuck yourself."

CHAPTER FIVE

TALLINN - KODU JANES

Goodbook arrived at the pre-arranged meeting place, a bar called Kodu-Janes that featured a painting of a bedraggled sad-eyed rabbit on a sign over the door. Before entering he stopped to take a good look around. The street was deserted, and a light misty rain was falling. Earlier in the day they had chosen this bar for a rendezvous after leaving the casino. Typically, when they were working they would leave the casino separately and meet up later.

They chose this bar primarily because of its location in Tallinn's Old Town, a couple of streets back from the Raekoja Plats, a square in the centre of town where in mid-summer hundreds of Swedes and Finns would make the pilgrimage across the Baltic Sea to sit in the midnight sun and drink beer all night at one of the many bars around the square. Kodu-Janes was in a narrow cobbled street that had several other alleys and streets leading from it, which made it a good place to escape from if the need arose. They also liked the fact that in the middle of the main room there was a fire exit door which opened with a push-bar onto yet another alley in the laby-rinth that was the Old Town and very handy for a quick exit as well.

Goodbook entered and stood just inside the door to take in the scene. The place was about half full, perhaps twenty customers in all, mostly seated at a mix of tables and wooden booths around the room. The conversation was animated, and the music loud! On the wall behind a brightly lit bar counter, in the centre of an array of spirits and liquor bottles, was another image of the bedraggled rabbit, its sad eyes gazing mournfully across the room.

Door was already there and Goodbook was pleased to see that he was sitting at a table next to the fire exit. He was conversing with a pretty girl holding a tray full of drinks.

Goodbook eased his sizeable frame past her, being careful not to knock the tray as she put two drinks on the table. He sat down next to Door, his back to the wall.

"Jules," said Door, "this is the lovely Lena who speaks four languages. Amazing! Got you a local beer, is that okay or you want something else?" he asked, continuing to gaze at Lena as he spoke.

"Nah mate, beer's fine" said Goodbook, taking a sip and getting froth on his moustache. He looked up and said "hi" to Lena who smiled back. She was wearing a very short black skirt and a T-shirt with the words 'It's Hard in Tallinn!' on the front and Goodbook could clearly see the outline of her breasts and nipples through the shirt.

She leaned over Door, "Do you like anything else please?" Door gave her his biggest smile and said, "Yes, what time do you finish tonight?" almost in a whisper.

She put her free hand on her hip and swayed a little, keeping time with the background music. "Well, I finish around five and then I meet my boyfriend and we go for swimming in the sea," she said, leaning over so her face was now very close to Door's face. "You like to come with me?" she continued, rocking her head from side to side, grinning at him.

Door looked sideways at Goodbook who was sipping his beer and seemingly not taking any notice of their conversation. "Oh yes, I would like to come with you," said Door, pausing to sip his beer but keeping his eyes on her, "but not with your boyfriend there – perhaps another time?" He stood up and kissed her lightly on the cheek and she smiled back. She looked back at Goodbook and gave him a little wave as she moved off to the next table, delivering drinks from her tray, chatting with the customers. On the back of her T-shirt was a picture of the same mournful rabbit as was hanging over the bar, with the words, 'Kodu-Janes .... A New Kind of Pub'

Door sat down, his eyes still on Lena, and turned to face Goodbook. "Watcha think?" he asked, "ain't she just cute as a button? Think she's playing hard to get?" Goodbook took a long pull at his beer before answering.

"Mate, this is good beer! She is cute and she ain't hard to get if I'm any judge, probably had more pricks than a second-hand dartboard!" He leaned closer to Door and dropped his tone of voice, "Mate, what happened tonight, they made you pretty soon back there?"

"I don't know, maybe I got a little quick – did you see me quick?" "No, couldn't see anything wrong, actually you were going well I thought. Maybe they got a pic of you, you think?"

Door sat back a little and drank some beer while he considered this. His picture had been circulated throughout the US casinos after he was spotted by Casapinta at the Oceanic in Atlantic City about a year back, but he did not believe that surveillance teams around the US, who shared information on crews, would have contacts around Europe that they would bother to share with. London for sure, Monte Carlo perhaps, but these pissy little casinos in the back arse of nowhere? It was because of his supposed anonymity in Europe that he and Goodbook found themselves in Tallinn, at the start of their 'tour' of Europe.

He put the beer down and leaned forward, conspiratorially, close to Goodbook. "Did you manage to cash out, you got the dough?"

"No worries," said Goodbook, "right here in me sky." He tapped his hip pocket. "Just over eight hundred bucks. Would have liked a bit more time to make some more though." Door shifted his position again, his face close to Goodbook's now. "Are you sure they made me?" he said, his voice almost a whisper.

Goodbook put down his glass. "Mate, I think so. Anyway, you saw the suits, seemed to me they were heading for you!"

Door sat back again, nodding slightly but turning to smile at Lena as she passed by on her way back to the bar counter. He looked at Goodbook. "Do you know what I'm thinking?" he asked. "I'm thinking we need to find out if they have a picture of me or if they just got lucky on the CCTV. We need to know cos if they do have a pic we need to re-boot our European idea, big time. If they have one probably all the casinos in Europe do as well." He gulped the rest of his beer and waved his hand, trying to catch Lena's eye.

Goodbook tugged Door's arm, "and how do you propose we find out?" he said, "Just go back there and ask them perhaps, or break in to the surveillance room and see what they got?"

"That's exactly what I have in mind, we go back when they close and break in. These pissy little casinos don't have proper security, it's a cinch!"

"These *pissy little casinos*," said Goodbook, mimicking Door's American accent, "don't need security cos they're run by the fucking local Mafia, that's why."

Door finally got Lena's attention again and ordered more beers. Goodbook called out to her, "Miss, bring me a Jack Daniels too please." He turned to Door, "We don't need to do anything, even if they have your pic, which I doubt. Can't see your US lot being in touch with these guys. Your average yank don't even know where Australia is on the map, never mind a former Soviet Bloc country like Estonia, or Latvia or Uzbekistan!"

"Uzbekistan?" said Door, "where the fuck is that?"

"Yeah, exactly, rest my case!" said Goodbook, smiling a little as the tension building in their conversation began to subside. "I think they just rumbled you, that's all, you're very good you are, but you're not perfect and they just got lucky – for sure it wasn't the inspector or the dealer, they never cottoned on to you."

"Okay," said Door, over-tipping Lena as she put the drinks on the table. "So what now? Obviously we have to move on, they'll probably circulate the tape to the other casinos here. How many are there, six?"

"Yeah, six or seven, but again I doubt they'll have that sort of network around here. The competition's fierce and if some crew fleeces someone else's place I'm sure they'll be happy with that!" He drank some beer, taking a good look around the room and focusing on two men entering the bar. Satisfied they were not the suits from the Viceroy he resumed talking to Door. "You're right, we maybe should leave town. That's the trouble with these small places, we might bump into those Viceroy goons just sitting here." He picked up the Jack Daniels and fished out the ice cubes, dropping them on the floor, and drank the bourbon in a single go. He wiped his mouth with the back of his hand and then wiped his hand on his shirt. "We need to move on and sort of stay low for a while. Fly below the radar. Just in case your pic is circulated."

Door looked at him, his beer glass poised halfway to his lips, "What? Stop working?" he said, his eyes wide. "You're kidding. Just quit cos we were made in this one horse town. You said yourself they probably won't circulate my pic. Alright, maybe we should leave Tallinn, but stop working?"

Lena appeared again by Door's side, leaning over so her face was close to his. "You like more drinks please?" she said, smiling her biggest smile. Door looked at Goodbook who nodded. "Ah yes, the same again please Lena." As she moved off, he called her back, "Lena, can I ask you something?" She smiled, returning to his side, waiting expectantly, still swaying to the music. "Can I get that T-shirt?" he said, pointing at her.

"Yes, I will bring you one from the bar, they are one hundred Kroons"

"No, no, I want this one," he said, squeezing the fabric lightly with his thumb and forefinger. She looked at him, tilting her head to one side as she considered his words. She giggled, swaying ever more. "Okay, then this one will cost you three hundred Kroons," and she turned to move away but Door caught hold of her hand.

"That's great" he said, beaming, "but I want it now!"

The smile froze on her face, and she stopped swaying and looked closely at him, her head tilted as she thought about it. A few seconds passed and then she smiled again. "Okay, but this will cost you a thousand Kroons." She put the tray down on the table and held her right hand out, palm up.

Door opened his wallet and placed two five hundred Kroon notes on her hand. She folded the money and placed it under an empty glass on her tray. Taking both hands to the hem of her T-shirt in one movement she pulled the shirt over her head and handed it to him.

He stood up, grinning, and kissed her lightly on the cheek. Around the room people started clapping and cheering. Lena picked up her tray and sauntered back to the bar counter, waving her free hand and curtseying to the crowd, like a prima ballerina taking a first-night ovation, totally un-fazed by the fact she was naked from the waist up!

Door sat down, clutching the T-shirt and holding it to his nose. He looked at Goodbook and smiled. "It's still warm," he said, his smile becoming a smirk.

"Mate, of course it's still bloody warm. Nice display you put on there, that's how we keep a low profile when we're working in a strange town! Great stuff." He sat back in his chair, arms folded across his chest, not amused.

"Oh, come on Jules," said Door, punching Goodbook lightly on his arm, "it's just a bit of fun, a trophy, a souvenir of Tallinn." He grinned.

"Ninety bucks for a bloody T-shirt, some souvenir you got."

"Jules, you can't tell me it wasn't worth that just to see her tits."

Goodbook sighed, relaxing a little, a smile spreading across his face." Yeah, maybe you're right Cliff my boy, maybe you're right. Nice pair. One thing's for sure, it's never dull, never dull."

Lena returned with their drinks wearing a different colour T-shirt but with the same wording and picture. Door pointed at the picture of the rabbit over the bar. "So, Kodu Janes means rabbit, no?"

Lena smiled at him, "No, it means a tame hare!" She placed the drinks on the table. "These are my treat, enjoy," she said with a smile and blew him a kiss with a little wave as she left their table.

Door watched her go, all the way back to the counter before he turned back to Goodbook. "Jules, d'ya really think we have to leave Tallinn? It's just starting to get interesting here."

"Listen, my tame hare friend, that Lena will have you on a lead soon," he said, laughing. "I do think we should leave town though, probably the best bet."

Door drew circles with his index finger around the top of his beer glass, which gave out a ringing sound. "Okay, we move on, but we can't stop working."

Goodbook leaned close to him "No, not stop, just modify our MO. A night here, a hit there, moving around like a small holiday, paying our way." He took another sip of his beer. "Then, what would be good is if we were to find a new casino, you know, brand new, just opening with a rookie team in surveillance, you know how it is. Opening night, big fuss, nervous staff. For the next few days everything's a bit rocky, all new security. Piece of cake for a man of your talents to just go in there, make a serious hit and clean 'em out." He sat back and finished his beer, looking at Door with his best smile. "Watcha fink?" he said, in a poor attempt at a New Jersey accent.

Door sat back and smiled at him. "Sounds good. Too good. Judging by your stupid grin you've got this all worked out, you know where there's a new casino opening. Am I right? You got it all figured?"

Goodbook beamed, "You got me Cliff, I know just the place — great climate, friendly people — speak English, casino opening soon."

Door raised his eyebrows. "And where is this Nirvana, might I ask?"

Goodbook pulled out a map of Europe from his back pocket, folded it this way and that and held it up. He pointed first at Tallinn, on the Baltic coast, then traced his finger down through Europe without pausing, past the shape of the boot that is Italy, making a circle around the island of Sicily, all the while grinning like the Cheshire Cat, before finally bringing his finger to rest on a tiny speck of an island between Sicily and Africa in the Mediterranean Sea.

"Malta."

CHAPTER SIX

ATLANTIC CITY – THE MARINA

From where he stood at the window of the Meadowlands offices, Browning had an unobstructed view of the rows of pontoons in the marina below. Perhaps a couple of hundred sailing yachts and cabin cruisers bobbed and swayed to the wind's gusty tune, while the late morning sun played hide and seek with scuttling clouds, their shadows gliding over the boats, the sudden changes of light dramatising their movement on the water.

Most of the berths on the pontoons were occupied and Browning wondered just how often any of those boats were actually used by their owners, apart from entertaining on deck while moored in the marina.

"Do you ever do any sailing?" The question came from Philip Meadows who had quietly entered the room where Browning was waiting. He turned back from the window and smiled at Meadows, shaking his head slightly, "Not really, never seemed to find the time."

Meadows was taller than Browning expected, almost his own height, dressed casually in slacks and an open shirt, jacket folded over his arm. Taking a step towards him Browning held out his right hand and said, "Doug Browning, Mr Meadows, how do you do?"

"Good Doug," Meadows replied, shaking Browning's outstretched hand. "Sorry to keep you waiting, won't you come into my office?" he said, turning to open an ornate carved wooden door and motioning Browning to enter. Browning turned to the girl sitting at the desk in the outer office where he had been waiting and nodded to her, mouthing a silent, "Thank you". She smiled.

Meadows's office seemed fairly big to Browning, more like an airline lounge than a workplace, with sofas and several big glass coffee tables with fashion and boating magazines scattered on and underneath them. Deep pile scatter rugs, prints, photos, and paintings hung at random with Tiffany lamps positioned to bring colour to the room. The small work-desk adjacent to the door seemed almost like an afterthought, not the kind of desk Browning had imagined he would find in the office of an iconic businessman whose name was synonymous with billion-dollar deals.

One side of the room was simply a floor to ceiling window overlooking the marina. Glass sliding doors opened onto a terrace boasting cane sofas, lounges and a large oblong table with several chairs. The floor of the terrace was laid in teak strips, much like a boat deck. Browning figured that was the idea, as being on the terrace had the feel of being on a boat. The offices occupied the entire first floor of a two-storey building standing alone on the west side of the marina. The terrace faced east and ran the entire side of the building, looking out over the pontoons to the entrance of the Senator Frank S. Farley State Marina, as it was officially called. Beyond that the inlet and the Atlantic Ocean. On the ground floor of the building were a number of small retail outlets, including a chandlery store and a yacht brokerage.

When Browning had arrived earlier in a cab, he checked the address with the cab driver before letting him drive off. Somehow he expected that the Meadows empire would be housed in a business tower, probably taking up two or three of the top floors, rather than in the very modest looking building he now found himself in.

Meadows led Browning out onto the terrace and they sat, facing each other across the table. "It's a little breezy out here today but the wind direction is such that we should be sheltered enough, is that alright with you Doug?" Browning nodded. "Works fine for me," he said, taking in the views.

At this moment the girl from the outer office appeared with a tray of coffee and pastries.

"Help yourself," said Meadows, whispering something to the girl before she left.

"Thanks," said Browning, pouring coffee from a Thermos jug into a mug emblazoned with the motif 'Meadowland Entertainment'. He looked at Meadows as he sipped the coffee. "It's a privilege to meet you Sir," he said, "but why am I here?"

Meadows smiled. "Straight to the point, eh? The guys at the Oceanic said you were very up-front. I need someone to take on a new casino project and Derek Harmon said he thought you would be right for the job, given your background and experience in other countries." He picked up a plate of pastries and offered them to Browning who declined. Meadows poured himself some coffee before continuing. "So, I wanted to meet you to get a feeling for you, find out what makes you tick, if you follow me," he said, smiling, "which is why I asked for you to come over here today. And, I appreciate your being here as I understand it's your day off."

Browning shook his head "Not a problem Sir, my pleasure."

"Do you call everyone Sir?"

"Pretty much I guess, people I don't know very well. It goes with the job, dealing with the public all the time. 'Sir' is an acceptable way to address people in most situations."

"Well, perhaps you could call me Philip," said Meadows, "I would prefer that."

"Okay Philip, you're the boss!"

"Actually I'm not, Derek Harmon is still your boss, I'm just the majority owner of the Oceanic." Browning was intrigued by the use of the word 'just', as if owning more than half of a billion dollar operation was hardly worth mentioning.

"Sorry Philip, I understand that. Boss is more a figure of speech really. In casinos we mostly refer to more senior management as boss."

"Okay Doug, I just wanted to make the point that I am not going to be involved in the day to day running of the Oceanic," Meadows said. "That's down to Harmon and his management team, of which you are a part, and that's how it will continue to be. Talking of which, I understand you did a pretty good job the other night with that incident in the casino."

Browning frowned a little. "Well, I can't agree with you on that, sadly. I'm not very happy with how it turned out."

"Really? Why's that? The way I heard it you spotted some bad guys and caught one of them."

"That's the point though; we only caught one of them," Browning said, pausing to sip his coffee. "The other two managed to slip away and that's a let down, considering we had already alerted security and they were being tracked. And they just walked out!

We have their pictures now but it's unlikely they'll return. At least not unless they change their appearances, you know, a wig, tinted glasses, beard, etc."

"But you caught the runner. Is that right, a runner?"

"Yes, I caught the runner but without one of the others to hang the actual offence on it may have been a little tricky to prove that the runner did anything wrong. We have a tape of the decoy passing the chips to the runner, but he could say, in the absence of the decoy, that it was money owed to him and he knew nothing about how it was acquired. Whereas if we have them all in for questioning then typically, when the going gets tough, one of them will give the others up in return for some sort of deal, a let-off perhaps, or a suspended sentence." Browning smiled at Meadows and continued, "There is no such thing as honour among thieves, don't let anyone tell you different."

"Interesting Doug, very interesting. So, you let the runner go with just a warning?"

"Well, there was some debate about charging him for assault or intent to harm but in the end he was the only one who got hurt, plus it was the sort of thing that wouldn't overly impress the cops, being called in for a minor incident! So we let him go, with a barring notice, not allowed to return to the Oceanic, ever. But he will of course. Been caught before, will be caught again. Creatures of habit these people, like moths round a flame."

Meadows looked at him for a few moments before speaking again, "Doug, how did you know the runner was a man before you took off his wig?"

Browning smiled. Meadows had done his homework. "Have you seen the security report on the incident?" he asked.

Meadows shook his head "No, Harmon filled me in on what happened, but I just wanted to hear it from you, how you worked it out."

"Well," said Browning, "it was a combination of things really. Short girls typically don't wear low heeled shoes, as this one did; they wear really high heels when they are out on the town. But men who wear women's high heeled shoes always find walking a bit tricky, especially on the sort of heavy duty thick pile carpet we have on a casino floor. This particular guy was having problems even with not-so-high heels." He looked at Meadows who continued to watch him intently, hanging on to every word he was saying.

Browning continued "Also, the clutch handbag was close to, but not exactly the same shade of blue as the dress. I mean enough not-the-same that any fashion conscious girl wouldn't wear them together. The bag itself was fairly small, so it accentuated the hands. Even the best drag queens still have giveaway men's hands, and he was gripping the bag rather than wearing it, if you see what I mean. Women spend their entire lives carrying handbags, it's second nature to them. They don't hold their bags, they wear them. Did you ever notice a guy in a fashion store waiting for his wife or girlfriend outside the changing rooms, grinning self-consciously and awkwardly holding her handbag? That's the difference. Also, he made a mistake wearing a dress. Trousers would have been better, because men's legs never quite look the same as a female's, no matter how smoothly shaved they are. It's a muscle thing. So anyway, that's part of how I got onto him being a man, stuff like that!" He paused to take another sip of coffee "Plus the fact that the wig was not sitting right, it was slightly off centre. Easy to spot really."

Meadows smiled. "Easy for you to say, I would never have seen any of those things."

"But it's part of my job," said Browning, "we're trained observers if you like. A British journalist once described London casino staff as 'Earth-bound Hawks' and it sort of struck a chord within our industry. It served to make people even more aware of the need to observe what's going on around you in casinos, not just on the gaming tables. So, we became people watchers as well as game watchers. We notice everything! Does that make sense?"

"Earth Bound Hawks," said Meadows, "I like that. Sounds like a rock band but it makes sense." His attention turned to something happening behind Browning and he stood up to see better. Browning turned to follow Meadows' gaze and saw a large Cabin Cruiser, maybe a 60 or 70 footer he guessed, leaving the nearest pontoon, the man at the controls on the fly-bridge waving in their direction. Meadows returned the wave and sat down again. He nodded towards the boat. "One of my fishing buddies. You ever do any fishing Doug?" he asked. Browning smiled, shaking his head "Not really, never seemed to find the time."

Meadows nodded "Was there anything else which gave the runner away to you, so you knew for sure it was a man?" Browning continued to watch the cruiser as it turned away from them, heading for the ocean. Bloody big boat to go fishing with. He was somehow intrigued by the idea of Meadows having fishing buddies. He had always thought of billionaires as being loners and had already put him in that category. Maybe it was time for a re-think.

He turned back to face him. "Well, when I got close to the runner at the cage I recognised him — blonde wig, sexy voice and all — as Pierre Breton, a small-time loser from Montreal or somewhere up there, French Canadian. As I said we know him of old, caught him before. This is probably why he was in drag unless it was a turn on!" He grinned at Meadows. "But I recognised his eyes. You can change your hair, make up your face, grow a moustache, shave off your beard, even have plastic surgery, but your eyes stay the same. Even coloured contact lenses don't change them enough. Mind you I was surprised to find him working with a team. Had him figured for a lone wolf really, you know, an opportunist, steal a handbag here, filch a few chips there, that sort of thing. He wouldn't give up the team though, which also surprised me, given what I said before about no honour among thieves. Maybe he was just too scared to give them up."

"Scared?" asked Meadows, "scared of what?"

"Scared of them. The crew."

"Where did you pick up this thing about the eyes?" said Meadows. "Was that part of your casino training?"

"Not really," said Browning, "but over the years I came into contact with plenty of police detectives and they're all tuned into the technique. Eye recognition that is."

Meadows nodded, seemingly deep in thought, then suddenly leaned forward, both hands on the table, looking intently at Browning's face, "Tell me Doug, was it really necessary to hit him?"

"Yes."

"Why?"

"Because it was the only sure way to disarm him safely, to incapacitate him."

"How did you know he had a can of mace?"

"I didn't, just knew he had a weapon. Instinct. Could've been a knife."

"But you knew him of old. Was he ever violent previously?"

"No."

"But you still felt there was danger"

"Yes."

"So you took him out, just to be sure?"

"Yes."

"And you were certain you would incapacitate him with just one punch?"

"Pretty sure, yes."

"And would you still have thrown the punch if you didn't know it was a man, but thought it was a woman?"

"Correct," Browning replied. He sensed that this was a significant moment and a test perhaps in Meadows' scrutiny and evaluation of him. "Do you have a problem with that Philip?" Now it was Browning's turn to gaze intently and the two men maintained eye contact without speaking for what seemed to Browning a long time. And then Meadows smiled. "No, not at all Doug, not at all. Are you free for lunch?"

CHAPTER SEVEN

ATLANTIC CITY - GARDNER'S BASIN

As they left his offices, Meadows asked Browning to wait in the lobby whilst he went to get his car. Browning was surprised as he was expecting a limo and a driver, don't know why, he thought, don't all rich guys have drivers? It occurred to him that by the minute Meadows was becoming less like the typical billionaire he had imagined; be interesting to see what car he drives, a Lexus perhaps, Porsche, sporty Merc? He made a bet with himself that it would be a small, top of the range BMW — probably an M3 saloon or something like that, maybe a Z4, bright red!

Right on cue Meadows drew up outside in a dark green Ford Ranger pickup truck. Might be brand spanking new Browning was thinking, with chrome running-boards and silver-alloy wheels, but it's a pickup truck just the same!

Browning climbed in, smiling broadly. "Something funny?" asked Meadows. "No, not really, just not expecting you to be driving a pickup!"

"Well, what did you expect?"

"Dunno really, Lexus, Porsche, Beamer perhaps. Is this your only car?"

"Why, you don't like this one?"

"No, not at all, I mean, yes I like it, it's not that I dislike it, just surprised that this is your ride," said Browning, clipping up his seat belt. "Typically, guys like you seem to drive around in the top marques, not Fords anyway, and not pickups. Seems I got it wrong. I always tell my guys that assumptions are dangerous, and here I am doing it myself." He looked over to Meadows as the pickup began to move off, "I hope I haven't offended you Philip."

"No, you haven't, but I am curious about 'guys like you', what do you mean by that exactly?"

"Well, you know, iconic businessmen, entrepreneurs, so-say billionaires. I can't see Trump driving himself around, much less in a Ford pickup."

"What about Bill Gates, you can't see him driving around in a pickup either?"

Browning smiled. "Ah well, Gates, hmmm, yes maybe you're right, perhaps he would drive himself around, in a battered old Chevy probably!" he said, grinning now. "Powered by eco-fuel though, or solar panels, that would be it."

Meadows smiled but remained silent as he concentrated on making a left turn. As the pickup gathered speed he looked briefly at Browning, "What sort of car do you drive Doug? Let me guess, a restored seventies Mustang, maybe a Charger, Stingray perhaps. I see you in one of these classics. Am I right?"

"Actually, I don't drive, so I haven't got a car, get cabs everywhere."

"You don't drive. Amazing," said Meadows, shaking his head. "I think you're the only adult I ever met that can't drive!"

"I can drive, I just don't."

"You can but you don't. You choose not to. Why's that?"

"Philip if you don't mind, I don't really want to get into that right now. Is that okay?"

"Sure, no problem," said Meadows, raising his eyebrows. He checked both wing mirrors before making another left turn. "We're almost there now," he said, "do you know this area?"

Browning glanced around as if looking for a familiar landmark. "I saw a sign back there saying 'Welcome to Gardner's Basin' but it looks to me as if we're still pretty much in the marina. We haven't come very far, and I see some yachts over there. Otherwise no, I don't know this area."

Meadows parked outside a narrow two-storey wooden building. An oval yellow sign perched on a pole announced 'Back Bay Ale House' in letters written around a shamrock. A large balcony stuck out from the side of the building, perched on timber support beams. Browning thought the whole place looked odd. The roof on the porch was painted green, the balcony roof was red, the wooden façade of the structure was brown. It looked unfinished, the balcony an afterthought, a whimsical addition. The place was fairly busy with perhaps twenty or more people that Browning could see, scattered around on the porch and on the patio. And this a mid-week day and not yet twelve thirty.

"Welcome to the Ale House," said Meadows, walking up the steps to the porch, "the home of the Basin Mason Margarita!" Crossing the porch, he opened the door to the building and held it open for Browning to enter. Inside a small hallway a steep wooden staircase rose to the first floor. On the walls were dozens of prints, pictures, paintings and memorabilia; a round wooden sign proclaimed, 'Whitbread Ales', a painting of a tea clipper, photos of groups of smiling people wearing 'Back Bay' T-shirts. A voluptuous mermaid, sitting with her tail looped under and wearing two scallop shells as a bra, gazed at Browning from a print that proclaimed that the Ale House was indeed, as Meadows had said, 'the home of the Basin Mason' although there was no mention of a Margarita! In fact, the mermaid was holding a large glass of beer. "Interesting place," said Browning, climbing the stairs ahead of Meadows.

They came to a small dining room with eight or nine small, square tables that were adorned with pinkish-purple shiny plastic tablecloths. The walls were bare save for mirrors placed here and there and although daylight came in from some narrow sash windows, he found the room a little gloomy.

"You come here a lot?" said Browning. Meadows just smiled back at him and led the way outside to the terrace and sat down at a corner table, his arm over the railing, looking very much at home and at ease. Browning sat opposite him, seeing another clue to the Meadows persona, this quirky out of the way place, a restaurant that feels like a pub. Certainly not the sort of place he imagined that the mega-rich would gather to be seen for lunch! Looking around he realised they were now sitting on the balcony he saw from outside, jutting out from the side of the building. There were five or six other tables, but they were all empty. He could see right across the marina to the Meadowland offices and the Trump Resort. Beyond them two large buildings dominated the skyline.

Following his gaze Meadows said, "The taller building on the left is the Borgata and next to it is the Water Club Hotel, all part of the same complex. But I guess you know that already!"

"I recognise them, but I haven't been to the Borgata, or any other casino here actually."

"Really" said Meadows, surprise in his voice "You've been here three years and never visited another casino, not checked out the opposition?"

More homework thought Browning. I never told him I've been here three years.

"No, I'm only interested in what we do at the Oceanic, not interested in what all the others do. When I'm off duty I have better things to do than visit other casinos."

"Interesting Doug," said Meadows, "although I am surprised. So, what do you do in your free time then, if you don't mind?"

"Not at all. I do some martial arts, box a little, work out, read a lot. Most of all I walk."

"Walk?"

"Walk" He nodded to emphasise the point. "Along the Boardwalk, the beach, around the parks, I like to walk. It's my way of chilling out."

"You continue to surprise me, Doug. Met lots of joggers but never a walker!" said Meadows, making a tent with his fingers. "And you me," said Browning "Your offices, your car, this place, not your typical rich and famous lifestyle."

Meadows smiled and turned to wave at a waiter. "Do you fancy a drink before we order?"

"Perrier water please."

"You don't want to try their beer? It's pretty good."

"No, I don't drink alcohol so the Perrier will be just fine."

"You don't drink?" said Meadows. "More surprises. Not ever?"

Browning smiled at him, shaking his head. Amazing how people always seemed to react with astonishment to the news that he did not drink, as if they had never met anyone like that before, must be from a different planet, different species even.

The waiter arrived carrying a pitcher of water and two glasses which he set down and filled with water before he spoke. "Good morning gentlemen, my name is James, and I will be your waiter today. Can I get you a drink before your meal perhaps?" James was a large bald guy with a goatee beard. Browning thought he knew him from somewhere. The Oceanic perhaps.

"Thanks James. A Perrier for my guest and my usual beer please," said Meadows. "Yessir Mr Meadows, be right back with the menu," replied James, and he was gone.

"Borgata," said Meadows, nodding again towards the complex across the marina "It means 'Little Village.' You know Doug, names and brands are so important. They built that facility, complete with a casino, a spa and even another hotel in the same complex and looked around for a name to rival Bellagio. What did they come up with? Borgata! Now Bellagio, there's a name to conjure with." He said it again, almost in a whisper now. "Bellagio, Bellagio." He smiled at Browning. "Point is, it's a romantic name, mysterious. The soft G allows one to extend it, draw it out. It just rolls off the tongue."

Browning had a vision of Giulia, soft G in her name, lying naked on the bed in their room in the Hotel Suisse. Through the open French windows, Lake Como sparkled in the August sun. A zephyr of warm air blew in off the lake, teasing the lace curtains to dance and sway. Smiling, her slender arms outstretched, beckoning him, she whispered, "Caro, amante, leccimi di nuovo." He shook his head, back now in the Ale House to find Meadows still whispering,

"Bellagio". He looked across at Browning. "You ever been there Doug, Bellagio?"

"The one in Vegas, no," he said, "the one in Italy yes. A couple of days in a nice little hotel by the lake. Meeting the locals, picking up the language. You know."

"Yes, a lovely place. Charming. But now consider Borgata," he said, his voice returning to normal pitch, "just the word Borgata." He emphasised the hard G. "Sounds like something an Italian waiter would say under pressure." He mimicked "Where's-a my dessert-a for a table Uno?, I'm-a waiting a for it, Borgata, Borgata — dis-a place, mamma mia where's-a my dessert-a?" He smiled at Browning "See what I mean? You follow me?"

Browning laughed. "Dats-a very good," he said, continuing the mimic as Giulia appeared before him again, laughing at his attempts to speak Italian.

James returned to their table with the drinks and startled Browning out of his reverie. "May I tell you about our specials today?" said James, continuing without waiting for a reply. "Everything on the menu is good to go but we don't got any Delmonico today." Meadows pulled a face, but James seemed not to notice. "Also, we don't got any soft shell crabs. Special fish entrée today is Mahi Mahi, plain grilled over charcoal and served with sticky rice and a mango papaya salsa." He looked at the two men. "Just give us a couple of minutes please," said Meadows. James nodded and moved away.

"What's Delmonico?" asked Browning, opening the menu.

"It's probably the best steak to be found anywhere in New Jersey. End cut of the rib, and they do it fantastic here, a favourite of mine." They were quiet for a moment, each looking through the menu. James re-appeared and Meadows ordered a flat iron steak and looked at Browning "You ready Doug or you need more time?"

"No, I'm good." He looked up at James. "I'll try the seafood Cobb salad please."

"Good choice gents," said James, gathering the menus before heading off.

"So where were we?" said Meadows.

"Power of brands and names, Borgata versus Bellagio"

"Ah yes. Well anyway, that's my slant on it, branding is so important, mostly people don't realise, even so-say marketing hot shots. Oceanic is a good example, it's up there on the Boardwalk and just along from it is The Taj Mahal! The Oceanic is actually a better facility than the Taj but outside of Atlantic City nobody has heard of it. But everyone knows that there's a Taj Mahal here, the whole world knows!"

"Are you thinking to re-brand the Oceanic?"

"Re-brand it? Now there's a thought. Before Harman took over it was more like the Titanic, business wise. Sinking," said Meadows, frowning. "Maybe we should call it the Titanic, how about that, it's a brand all of its own if you think about it."

Browning considered this. "Well, it's funny now you mention it, but I don't recall seeing the name used to brand anything, except the movie of course. I recently came across a South African entrepreneur who was going to build a replica of the Titanic with modern day kit, you know, radar, diesel turbines, computerised operations, a state-of-the-art cruise liner. He was peddling a casino on board and I was given the task of checking it out. He wanted five million for the concession plus rent plus a share. All that for a space on a boat that wasn't built yet. I couldn't see the value in it. Don't think he ever built it, I never heard any more about it."

"Was this when you were in working in South Africa Doug?"

"Yes, that's right. When I was at Sun City, near Johannesburg"

"And that's where you met Derek Harmon," Meadows said, a statement not a question.

"That's right, Derek was recruited from Vegas, The Venetian I think, to work his magic at Sun City. He came in and was like a breath of fresh air; compared to other guys I've worked for."

"What makes him so different?"

"Well, for a start he's not ego driven. He talks with his team not at them. When you work with Derek that's it, you work with him not for him. There's a genuine team spirit in the management at the Oceanic and that's how it was down there in Africa too. To be honest when he first arrived at Sun City I thought, "here we go, a yank, that's all we need. But I knew he was good from the very first HOD."

"HOD?" asked Meadows, tilting his head to one side.

"Head of Department meeting. Derek has them every week. We all meet up and talk about what's happening, the results, what promotions are coming up, ideas, you know, a sort of forum where the various departments update everyone with how things are in their area of the operation. Food and beverage, table games, slots, keno, security, surveillance, everyone is there, and we all pitch in."

"No one from the hotel?"

"No, typically the hotel operates in tandem with the casino. Except in some places where the hotel runs the f&b outlets located in the casino footprint."

"And what does your job entail exactly, Operations Shift Manager?"

Browning smiled and sipped at his water, wondering when the food was coming as he was hungry now. "Well, the OSM is like a ringmaster, is how I see it. You remember the 'Three Ring Circus' of Barnum and Bailey? Well, a casino is a bit like that. Over here the table games. In the middle the slots and the keno lounge. Over there the f&b outlets, bars, and restaurants. Flowing through it all are the dealers, slot techs, cleaners, security and surveillance, the staff canteen team and of course the players and other visitors to the facility.

"Other visitors to the facility?" said Meadows. "Who would they be Doug?"

"Well, you know, the police, fire department. People visiting in some official capacity. Paramedics now and again." Meadows nodded and Browning continued explaining his role. "So, the OSM's role is to ensure it all works according to plan. In the absence of the actual Department Head, I can enable or disable any decision made in all departments. My shifts are spent moving around the facility to keep an eye on things, stepping in as need be to resolve problems and issues that arise. A single point of authority for the various shift managers running the facility. Does all that make any sense?"

At this point James returned with the food. He left with the customary "Enjoy," and Meadows said, "yep," while milling black pepper all over his steak.

"Thanks for that Doug, I see it now. You may have thought that I knew how it all works but actually I didn't. I drive the marketing and financial sides of the business but the operation itself is a mystery to me, how it all comes together. How's the salad?"

"Looks good" said Browning, picking at the ingredients with his fork and carefully examining each item.

"Doug, you ever heard of a place called Malta?" asked Meadows, cutting into his steak.

"Malta? Yes, it's a small island in the Med. Near Italy."

"That's it. Great climate and popular with the Brits, so I thought you might know it."

"Never been there myself but a kid I was at school with in the UK lived there for a couple of years. His dad ran Barclays Bank in Malta. He seemed to like it but I remember he said there were hardly any trees on the island and no grass on the football pitches. Soccer that is. I couldn't picture it at the time, playing football on clay. Imagine!"

Meadows took a swig of his beer. "Well, I have a holding company doing a property development there with a local partner, which you need to have in some parts of Europe. Our Maltese partner owns a new casino soon to open there which is going pear-shaped and he's asked me for help. Would something like that be of interest to you perhaps?"

"What, go to Malta and sort it out?"

"Exactly. Your profile fits perfectly. I understand you have the experience, worked around the world and know your way around; you know lots of people in casinos and putting a team together shouldn't be a problem for you." Browning nodded without speaking, so Meadows continued. "I don't know exactly what's there right now, but it seems the whole project is in disarray, headless, no management. On another level I understand you are single, unattached, and have no ties here to prevent you from going. Is that right?" Browning nodded again so Meadows continued. "You also have a British passport, and with Malta being in the EU, a work permit is a formality. You could start right away if you agree to go."

"Just like that?" said Browning.

"Just like that"

"What about my job here? Do I have to give that up or would it be held open? I mean, how long do you have in mind for me to be out there?"

"To be honest Doug I haven't got that far along really. First thing I need to know is if you are willing to consider it. If you are then we will work out the nuts and bolts of the deal and your personal terms with Harmon. How's that?"

"Well okay in principle, I guess. But if I go, will I be working for the Oceanic or the local partner?"

"Neither. You would be on assignment to the local partner, but you would work for Meadowland, reporting directly to me. Meadowland will take on the operation of the casino on a management contract and you would be responsible for it overall. It's a setup we could think about mirroring elsewhere if this pans out alright. A satellite casino company outside the USA."

There's the carrot, thought Browning. Meadows put down his cutlery and pressed the palms of his hands together in an almost prayer-like gesture.

"It's small compared to the Oceanic of course Doug, perhaps twelve or fifteen gaming tables, maybe a hundred slots. Back at the office I have the floor plans and the design schematics. It will have a restaurant and bar, you know, like the small local casinos they have in England"

"Will it be a stand-alone casino or is there a hotel as well?" said Browning.

"It's in a new facility built in the grounds of an existing small hotel, which has recently been refurbished."

"Will the hotel operation fall under the Meadowland contract as well?"

"No, our local partner owns and operates the hotel, and he owns a few small hotels around the Island. Three-star units I'm told, mid-range."

"Okay, so how big is the hotel? Does it have a restaurant? What else is in the vicinity? Other hotels, restaurants, bars? Is it near the sea? Is there a tourist attraction nearby, what?"

"Whoa," said Meadows, holding both hands up, fingers outstretched.

"Just hang on there Doug, we can go through all this stuff back at the office but right now I just want to determine your level of interest to maybe take this on." He sat back in his chair and sipped his beer before continuing. "What I can tell you is that it's in a town called Mdina, in the centre of the island. It's a walled city set on the highest point in Malta."

"And the casino will be inside the walled city?"

"No, the hotel grounds are situated just outside the entrance to the city, which is mostly a pedestrian area, but it's close to an external parking area used by tourists and other visitors."

"Fancy that," said Browning, "Mdina, a walled city."

"I'm told the locals call it the Silent City!"

Browning munched at his salad, deep in thought. Eventually he looked up at Meadows.

"Okay Philip," he said, smiling, "let's see if we can't do this. The Silent City huh. Imagine that, a silent casino."

CHAPTER EIGHT

SLOVENIA - NOVA GARICA

Door walked into the lobby of the Perla Casino and looked around in amazement. He turned to Goodbook. "Wow, I didn't know they had casinos this big in Europe, never mind this pissy little town, where is it?"

"Nova Garica," said Goodbook, smiling. "Actually, it's one of the larger casinos in Europe and there's another one here almost as big, The Park, just across town"

"How do you know all this stuff anyway?"

"Google."

"So, what have we got here then?"

"About thirteen hundred slots and about seventy tables, mostly roulette and blackjack but they also got a craps table here, unusual for Europe." They wandered into the gaming area which was fairly busy in the late afternoon and Goodbook paused next to a group of roulette tables. He looked at Door with a serious look on his face. "Mate," he said, almost in a whisper, "we ain't gonna work this place, I think it's too risky, unless you want to play some honest blackjack."

"Well, I'm cool with that. Anyway, we agreed we would stick to smaller places on this part of our trip. So why are we here then?"

"Just for a look-see. Thought you might be interested to see a big operation like they have in the States, remind you of when you were a dealer." He beamed at Door, and they strolled by the blackjack area, finding a small bar next to the cash desk.

Goodbook perched himself on a high stool and waved at the barman before turning back to talk to Door who was still standing, watching a game of blackjack on a nearby table. "Mate, we're staying about 25 clicks down the road from here in a place called Kopar." The barman arrived and Goodbook ordered two beers.

"Why Kopar?" said Door, without turning his head away from the blackjack game.

"It's by the sea and has a marina. In fact, it's Slovenia's only access to the sea, but anyway because of the marina there's lots of short-let accommodation around and it's an easy drive to some other small towns that also have casinos. So, I figured we stay in Kopar for a couple of weeks or so and then head down south for Malta."

The barman arrived with the beers and Goodbook passed one to Door. "Jules, are you sure that pissy little car you hired will get us anywhere?" He smiled and took a pull at the beer. "Never heard of one of those before, a Skoda, what the fuck is that?"

"Mate you don't know nothing," he said, seemingly offended. "Skoda is a big seller in California, Australia, and Europe. A small, rugged car, a bit low on creature comforts, but user friendly, a real workhorse and cheap to run."

"Get out of here," said Door. "You make this stuff up as you go along. Couldn't we afford a Beamer or something a bit more chic? This is supposed to be a working holiday remember?" Goodbook put down his beer and wiped his moustache with his fingers. He pointed at Door, "Mate, I make the arrangements, remember, and you make the money. That's the deal!" He relaxed a little and smiled, "Anyway Cliff boy, you're far too good looking to need a flash car to get noticed. Not that your face won't get you into trouble one of these days, cos it will."

Door put his beer down on the bar counter and turned back to view the blackjack. "Mate," said Goodbook, "what's the attraction there, someone counting?"

"No," said Door, turning back to face him with a grin, "just a great bod on the girl inspecting the table. Super sexy she is." Goodbook rolled his eyes and let out a sigh.

"Here we go again. Time to go mate and sort out the apartment I got for us."

"If it's just a few clicks up the road, you can do that and come back for me."

"Why, so you can find out when she finishes," said Goodbook, nodding at the inspector who had taken Door's fancy. "Or so you can do some good old-fashioned card counting here and get yourself locked up." He finished the beer and left some notes on the counter. "Let's go mate."

"Aw Jules, it's just starting to get interesting. We did sod-all in Vienna and the train here was dull and boring. I wouldn't mind relaxing a little." Goodbook put a hand on each hip and stood close to Door. "Cliff boy," he said, with a big smile, "you're my mate and we're a good team but we don't, neither of us, go to casinos alone. You know that we agreed before. I ain't as young as you mate so I'm a bit tired and I'd like to go now. We still must pick up the keys for the apartment, then freshen up, get some groceries and stuff then get an early dinner somewhere. "Maybe a nice seafood joint by the sea if we're lucky." He raised his eyebrows, his hands still on his hips, and waited for the answer." Door shrugged his shoulders. "Okay Jules, Kopar it is," and led the way back to the lobby, pausing just long enough to give the blackjack inspector his biggest smile.

She blushed.

CHAPTER NINE

LONDON - SHEPHERD'S MARKET

As Browning left the lobby through the revolving doors, the doorman at the Park Lane Hilton gave him an expectant look and nodded towards the parked row of cabs waiting outside with their orange 'For Hire' lamps glowing dimly in the gloom of early evening. Browning smiled and shook his head as he turned to his right, walked past the Podium Restaurant then turned into Pitts Head Mews.

The street lamps flickered into life as he walked towards a small boutique hotel that was once an annex to the Hilton. He went through the arched passage at the side of the building into Shepherd Street, the heart of Shepherd's Market.

Comprising perhaps ten or twelve mews and several small streets in a triangular shaped area, squeezed in between Mayfair's Curzon Street, Park Lane and Piccadilly, this had once been an infamous 'red light' district known for its discreet brothels. With the advent of casinos in Mayfair in the late sixties and early seventies, property values in Shepherd's Market had soared and the brothels mostly moved away. Yet one or two had stayed under cover, got rid of the give-away red lights and moved up-market.

Browning knew the area very well, having worked at two casinos in Mayfair during his time in London at the Crystal Beach and The Stanhope. This area had a timelessness about it that appealed to him. In the years since he first came here, the cafés and pancake parlours had given way to nouvelle-cuisine restaurants with Michelin stars. Yet the pubs were still here; Ye Grapes, The Kings Arms, Shepherds Tavern. Now they were 'gastro pubs', up-market eating houses where cheap bar snacks had given way to extensive menus with restaurant prices. Terraced homes were now 'town houses' and fetched literally millions of pounds, hence the proliferation of high-end estate agents now to be found in the area.

Yet Shepherd's Market retained a certain quirkiness that Browning felt could not be found anywhere else in London. In the midst of these high-end restaurants and expensive houses there were still some 'open all hours' stores selling groceries, cheap wines and newspapers. Their offerings of cut flowers, fruit and vegetables were stacked in crates and boxes on the pavements outside. A hardware store showing pots, pans, plastic bowls and power tools on display in its window did not, somehow, look out of place. A Snappy Snaps shop offered a photo developing service, while across the street sat the Piccolo Bar, which was actually not a bar at all, but an alcohol-free café.

He turned up his collar in the damp cool air and walked slowly down Shepherd Street, pausing by Shepherd's Tavern where a group of hardy souls, driven outside by the recent smoking ban, stood on the corner of the street chattering, drinking, and smoking, oblivious to the cold air. The cobblestones in the road shone from an earlier shower as he continued towards the Kings Arms, taking it all in and feeling very much at ease being there. He wondered how the small shops survived, paying the sort of rents the area's top tier status must now command.

At the end of the street the lights of the Kings Arms beckoned, and he quickened his pace as misty rain swirled on a freshening breeze. Approaching the pub, he jostled his way through the inevitable group of smokers gathered on the pavement and went inside. He spotted Shruggy immediately, perched on a high stool at the bar. Their eyes met and Shruggy jumped off the stool and opened his arms wide. "Hello Duggie, good to see you sunshine."

"And you too me old son," said Browning, stepping forward and putting both arms around his friend. The two men stood still for a moment in a warm embrace, then Shruggy returned to his stool with Browning standing alongside him. They grinned at each other, Shruggy's head tilted to one side, as was his manner.

"You still on the wagon?" said Shruggy, beckoning to the barman.

Browning nodded.

"What can I get you then, a Coke?

"No, I'll have an orange juice." He looked at the barman. "No ice please."

"Same again for me Bert," said Shruggy, pointing at his half empty beer glass.

Browning looked at Shruggy. They had known each other for years and worked together in casinos in London and Africa, becoming good friends along the way. Back then Raymond Shoulders had long hair, a body builder's physique, and a habit of shrugging his shoulders during a conversation, particularly when emphasising a point. Hence the nickname. The long hair had mostly gone, as had the once enviable physique.

Shruggy looked at Browning. "I know what you're thinking Duggie."

"What's that then?"

"S'obvious innit, know what I mean?" He shrugged, smiling at Browning.

"What's obvious?"

"You're wondering how gorgeous Ray turned into this short, fat balding bloke!" He sipped his beer, then looked at Browning again. "Am I right?"

"Well no, unusually for you, you're wrong"

Shruggy seemed surprised. "Really, you don't see me that way?"

"No, I don't see you as short, fat and balding," said Browning, grinning now "but two out of three ain't bad!" He laughed and raised his juice. "Cheers Shruggy."

Shruggy smiled back. "Always the joker Duggie, some things don't change. What a pair we were, Duggie and Shruggy. Don't think we really knew what we had back then."

"Well," said Browning, raising his eyebrows, "as I recall a lot of people thought you were my dad!"

"Yeah, don't remind me. Although I was flattered that a good-looking bloke like you could be mistaken for one of mine!" He shrugged. "S'obvious innit, though when you think about it, age wise I could be your dad."

"How old are you now Shruggy? Sixty something?"

"Yeah, sixty-four, so that would make you?" He paused, took a swig of his beer and shifted on his stool. The two men looked at each other, a moment passed. "About forty I reckon, maybe forty-two, am I right?"

Browning tilted his head. "Just about. How long has it been since we caught up?"

Shruggy took a long pull at his beer, glancing around the pub as he did so. "Dunno really, I think the last time I saw you was just after you got the job at Sun City."

"After you got me the job at Sun City you mean," said Browning, smiling.

"Well whatever, you came over here for the casino show at Earls Court, like we always did. We went for a Ruby at that Indian gaff in Gloucester Road, bleedin' awful it was, remember?"

"Yeah, remember it well, I reckon that was six years ago."

Shruggy shrugged his shoulders and looked at Browning. "So, Duggie, what is it you want son? What can I do for you?"

"You still working?" said Browning, "or retired now?"

"Redundant, not retired. I went back to Les Royals a couple of years back, scored a job as an Executive Host, was going alright, then some Asian consortium took it over, to restore Les Royals to its former glory they said."

"And?"

"S'obvious innit, know what I mean? They got in some hot shot from France or Monaco to run the joint and next thing you know I'm too old. So, they made me redundant." He shrugged and waved to the barman.

"You didn't contest it, get a lawyer?"

"Nah, they gave me a decent payout and maybe they're right, maybe I am too old. Anyway, I couldn't be arsed with a lawyer and all that. At the end of the day, they're the only ones who make any money out of it."

The barman sidled up to them, wiping the bar top with a cloth. Shruggy finished his beer and ordered another. He looked at Browning. "More juice?" Browning nodded.

"So, never mind me Duggie, still dont know what you're after?"

"Ever been to Malta?"

"Malta," said Shruggy, smiling now. "Yeah, I been there, Valetta, years ago though! You remember when we was at The Stanhope? Well, there was that Maltese girl working there, coffee waitress, you remember her? Really long legs!"

Browning stroked his chin with his fingers. "Christine?"

Shruggy beamed at him. "That's her, Christine Apap was her name, and cut a long story short, we had a weekend together over there. Brilliant it was, great weather, great sex, good food, loved it!"

Browning raised his eyebrows. "Weren't you still married to Doreen then?"

"Well, I was, but we were effectively separated."

"Effectively?"

Shruggy shrugged. "S'obvious innit, know what I mean? We was still living together on account of my kid, you remember Jeanette, she's coming up twenty-six soon, where does the time go? Anyway, it was pretty much all over between us, me and Doreen, and I took off with this Christine. Her folks had a place over there, but they lived in Manchester. You can guess the rest, am I right?" Browning smiled and nodded.

"So anyway," said Shruggy, "tell me about Malta. You going there? Tired of Atlantic City?"

"No, no, I'm happy enough at the Oceanic but we have a new owner, Philip Meadows, and he wants me to set up this place in Malta." Browning sipped his juice. "Small operation, local partner in the frame who came to Meadows when Lloyd Baker, who they hired to set up and run the place, just walked out." Shruggie raised his eyebrows and looked at Browning as he sipped his juice. "Not surprised, I worked with Baker, what a dick. Is that the Philip Meadows who owns half of New Jersey, or some-such? Property developer."

Yeah, that's the one," said Browning. "Anyway, it seems that Baker set up a training school and ordered the equipment before he left, but I don't know much more than that right now. So, I'm going out there tomorrow for a few days to see what's what and then I'll have a better idea of how it will pan out."

"You got anyone lined up?" said Shruggie, tilting his head.

"Well, I asked the Head of Surveillance at the Oceanic to lend me Chas Casapinta, his number two, for a couple of months and I'd like to borrow a slots guy but that's about the only help I can call on from the Oceanic. You know Harmon. Runs a tight team and all that."

"Too true. I'm surprised he let you go to be honest. Be good if you can get good surveillance help though, you'll need it when you open cos every team in Europe will come a calling. S'obvious innit!" He shrugged and dismounted from the high stool and stretched his arms out in front of him, looking over to the door as a couple of men in chauffeur's uniforms entered, their peaked caps tucked under their arms. They smiled at Shruggie, nodding to him and he nodded back. "So, how can I help you? What are you after?" he said to Browning, turning to face him.

Browning called to the barman to bring another beer. He watched the two chauffeurs who had now joined a couple of girls that were sitting at a table by the window. He nodded in their direction. "Friends of yours? The short one looks familiar." Shruggie turned to look at the group. "Yeah, car jockeys from Les R. The tall one is a good bloke, been there for years. Don't know the other one so well but I seen him in here a few times, seems to me he has a bit of a problem with the booze." Browning raised his eyebrows at this remark. "Really?" he said, handing Shruggie his third beer in the time since he had arrived. He smiled at his friend. "Well, you know about such things!"

Shruggie held the beer, seemingly unsure whether to drink it or not. He shrugged and took a huge gulp of it, covering his top lip with froth. "You always were the thinker Doug, some things don't change! You don't see me for six years, you see me knock back a few beers and you're judging me. Am I right?" He tilted his head. "Well, that's okay cos I know you know I know my limits! Nothing's changed, I like a drink when I'm in the mood, just like you used to, but it has never affected my work." He drank some more beer, as if to make the point.

Browning smiled and put his hand on Shruggie's arm. "Raymond, Ray, I'm sorry, I didn't mean to get on your case, don't think that. I was ribbing you a bit is all. I just meant that you know everyone in this business, you don't just know them, you know about them, what makes them tick! You probably know half the people in this pub and how they behave when they're not here!" He shook Shruggie's arm gently. "You took me the wrong way. Of all the people you know I'm the one who would never doubt you."

Shruggie turned and re-perched himself on the high stool, looking intently at Browning. "I'm sorry too Doug, I'm a little on edge lately, putting a brave face on, but the reality is I'm totally pissed off by the way things have gone for me since I left Les R." He shrugged. "I'm bored stupid is all. And I do spend too much time in here and probably I *am* drinking too much."

"Well, if you're up for it, I can change all that," said Browning. "I told Philip I would need a wing-man, someone I could trust to back me up. Feel like doing some work for a change?"

He smiled at Shruggie, who smiled back with a frothy grin. "Like what?" he said, his head tilted now even more than usual. "Go to Malta with you and make you look good, running a mickey-mouse tinpot casino for some rich yank and a bunch of dagos?" he looked at Browning, waiting for his response, which seemed to take forever.

"Yeah, something like that!"

Shruggy beamed "Well, s'obvious innit? I'm in."

CHAPTER TEN

ST JULIAN'S - MALTA

Cliff Door was feeling good with the world, cigar in hand, glass of white wine at the ready, sitting outdoors in the moonlight and enjoying the view from their table on the terrace of a restaurant called Peppino's. Goodbook was sitting next to him at the table, rather than opposite, all the better to take in the view. The terrace, at the front of the restaurant, was elevated from street level and across the road, at a level below their vantage point, was another restaurant's terrace, only much bigger than the one where they were sat. Beyond that there was an expanse of water, an inlet perhaps two hundred yards long and maybe sixty yards wide that opened out into a large bay, beyond which lay the Mediterranean Sea.

"Well now, will you take a look at that?" said Door, beaming. "Now that's a view and a half. Enchanting!"

"Sure is mate, no argument there." Over the sea the moon was rising slowly, turning from an orangey-red to a luminous silver as it climbed higher into the sky. The two men gazed in awe as it cast a shimmering reflection over the sea. It seemed to be so close they could touch it. The bay, the inlet, bobbing fishing boats and small leisure craft moored there — all bathed in moonlight, almost as bright as day. Along the left-hand side of the inlet a mix of old and modern apartment buildings overlooked the water. Restaurants were positioned at various levels, some up high and others further down with waterfront terraces. People strolled along the quayside path, passing several boathouses where boats of different types and sizes, in various states of repair, sat outside on the hard.

Goodbook sighed and raised his glass in a silent toast to the vista. "It's magical Cliff my boy. A kaleidoscope of colour and light, the moon, the neon signs, the way they've lit the arches in the buildings, the lights from the restaurants — what a spot!"

"Kaleidoscope," said Door, as if he had never heard the word before. "Well now that's a big word for you after only two glasses of wine." He held his glass of wine in front of the moon, looking closely at it. "Are we drinking the same stuff?"

"I like the way they've done the lights along the path down there," said Goodbook, ignoring the ribbing from Door. He pointed to the street lights spaced out along the quay. "Victorian style they are, like the ones that used to run on gas. A guy came around every night to light them."

"Did he have to come back in the morning and put them out too?

"Yes mate, he did. Had a long pole with a thing like a bell on the end of it, and he would snuff out the flame. That's where the expression comes from. "Snuffed it, when someone pops their clogs."

"I didn't know that," said Door, grinning sideways at his friend. "So, what happened to the gas after he snuffed the flame out? Did it keep flowing out or did he have to shut it off?"

"I suppose there was a valve in the base of the lamp, and he would turn it off."

"Well, if he did that, why would he need a long pole to snuff out the flame in the first place?"

Goodbook turned on his chair to face Door, folding his arms across his chest. "Now listen mate," he said, tilting his head to one side, "don't come the raw prawn with me, I don't bloody know, all I know is 'snuffed It' comes from those days when they had gas lamps."

"Well, where does 'popped his clogs' come from then?"

"How the fuck should I know?" said Goodbook, his voice raising a pitch.

"But you're the expert on sayings, you've got millions of 'em," said Door, laughing. But Goodbook was glaring, and at that moment the waiter who had seated them and taken their orders, re-appeared with an ice bucket.

"Good timing." Door said to him then turned back to Goodbook. "Jules, don't get so wound up I'm just joshing with you. Anyway, I think you're all mixed up with candles. They have those snuffers in church for those long altar candles."

"I'll give you a long altar candle in a minute mate, right up your jacksie!"

"Anyway," said Door, "they're not Victorian, they're art deco, thirties style!" He put both his arms out, palms up. "Just joshing with you Jules, just joshing!"

The waiter was turning the bottle around in the ice and draping a napkin over its neck. Goodbook looked up at him

"What's this place called mate?" he said, waving his arm at the view.

"This bay is called Spinola, and beyond the breakwater is Baluta

Bay. This whole area is called St Julian's. This your first time in Malta?"

"It is," said Door, "and I think it's wonderful, knocked out I am."

"Thank you," said the waiter, "your food won't be too long, enjoy."

"Can't get over this view," said Door, pointing across the inlet. "Look over there, more restaurants and bars all along the promenade."

Goodbook took a big gulp of wine and wiped his moustache with the back of his hand.

"See that there mate, the Chinese restaurant, see it, the place with all the tables on the pavement?" Door nodded and Goodbook continued. "Well just along from it there's a pub called The Dubliner."

"And?" said Door

"And?" mimicked Goodbook. "And, well it's amazing that wherever you go in the world, anywhere, you will always find a Chinese restaurant, complete with yer genuine slopeheads in the kitchen, and you'll always find an Irish pub. Though not always with yer genuine paddies behind the bar. Amazing that, don't you think?" Door smiled, the menu open in his hand.

"Funny you mention that, cos you're right. Before I was a roulette dealer, way before casinos, I was in banking. So, one time my boss takes me to Ireland on a business trip, some boring conference as it turned out, but the good thing was, it was in Dublin."

He was distracted by three women coming up the stairs by the side of the terrace. As they approached the restaurant door he stood up and smiled at them. "Good evening ladies," he said, bowing ever so slightly. They smiled at him, looking slightly embarrassed, before entering the restaurant. Door sat down.

"Anyway," he said, "my boss says now we're in Dublin we must find a typical Irish pub and have a Guinness. Except being as he was from bum-fuck Ohio or somewhere he pronounced it, "gwine ess". So anyways, we go into this pub, and he says to me, 'Now look at her Cliff boy," eyeing the barmaid, "ain't she just the prettiest, typical Irish colleen you ever saw, those blue eyes, jet-black long hair?" Before I can answer, she says, "G'day mates, what can I getcha?" "The broadest Aussie accent you ever heard! Even worse than yours it was, turned out she was from Sydney."

"And?" said Goodbook, his head down in the wine list.

"I'm just agreeing with you about Irish pubs and paddies, is all," replied Door, feeling a little miffed that Goodbook seemed uninterested in his story. Goodbook looked up and smiled at him.

"Did you buy her T-shirt too mate?" Reaching into his back pocket he pulled out a passport and gave it to Door, who looked surprised.

"What's this?" he said, turning it over.

"This is your new passport, for the purposes of our trip here," said Goodbook.

Door opened it and held it open at the photo page and showed it to Goodbook. "Frank Burt? Who the fuck is Frank Burt?"

"You are."

"Burt? I don't want to be Frank Burt. It's boring. Why can't I have an alluring name, something smooth and sexy?

"Like what?"

Door considered this for a moment. "What about Hilton Bridges? I could see myself as a Hilton."

"Why not Bryce Bedwell? I can see you as a bed-well! That's a real identity you have there. Some bloke called Frank Burt really exists. He's probably running around the world right now. You're his clone, so to speak."

"Well, I hope he's not in Malta, probably not big enough for two Frank Burts," said Door. He stood up and held out his hand to the empty seat across the table.

"I'm Frank Burt," he said aloud, in a very deep voice, "and I'm a clone. How do you do?" He held out his right hand, shook an imaginary hand very firmly, and sat down again.

Goodbook looked around to see if anyone was paying them any attention, but they were alone on the terrace. "Never satisfied you're not, I should have got you that Bedwell, he was on the list."

Door tapped the passport in his hand. "Why do I need a fake passport anyway?"

Goodbook sighed. "Because in Malta the first time you go in a casino you have to show your passport for ID and to prove that you are over twenty-one. Funnily enough, if you're from Malta, you've got to be twenty-five to go in."

"How strange is that?" said Door, flipping through the passport. He looked at Goodbook and held it up.

"Jules this is really very good, even got stamps of places old Frankie Burt has been. How did you get this?"

"Mate, piece of piss for a wizened old ex-detective. Sorted them out in Copenhagen when you went to the Tivoli Gardens. Mind you these won't pass muster at an airport or an official immigration check," he said. He pulled another one from his pocket and tossed it to Door. "But, they'll get us into the casino alright."

Door opened the second passport and burst out laughing. "Renton Tinn?" he shook his head and repeated the name, "Renton Tinn, you cannot be serious!"

"What's wrong with it, may I ask? What's so funny?"

"Well, just say it."

"Okay," said Goodbook, "Renton Tinn."

Door guffawed, banging his hand and the table and spilling wine on the floor.

Goodbook shook his head in bewilderment.

Still grinning, Door pushed back on his chair and puffed lazily on his cigar, taking in the scene, watching the passers by in the street below. Goodbook gazed at the moon which had now risen almost directly above them. He could see craters on its surface. But he couldn't figure out what Door thought was so funny.

The three women who had arrived a few minutes earlier came out of the restaurant holding glasses of wine and sat at the table next to Goodbook and Door.

"Hi girls," said Door, rising from his chair. "How lovely you look this evening, is this a special occasion perhaps?" The women smiled at him and glanced at each other. Door hovered by their table, waiting. Finally, the tallest of the three spoke to him.

"No, not really, just a girls' night out," she said, a half-smile on her face. Door returned it with his biggest smile.

"And may I ask, are you all Maltesers?" They all laughed. He glanced at Goodbook who was also laughing.

The tall girl spoke again. "You're American right?" Door nodded. She continued, "Well, Maltesers are a kind of candy, and we are Maltese, not Maltesers." She smiled at him and one of the other women called out, "But we can be sweet, tah". Door smiled at them and sat down again as the waiter returned with their food.

"Sorry mate," Goodbook said to the waiter, "can I trouble you for a bottle of still water? Big one, two glasses, thanks mate." The waiter nodded.

"Jules, I have to tell you I think the hotel you picked is really good, cheap and cheerful, very clean, just to let you know, good choice, well done," said Door.

"No worries mate, that's the deal, I make the arrangements you make the money."

Door lifted his glass and turned towards the women on the next table. "Cheers girls." They raised their glasses and mumbled "Cheers" back at him.

Door turned back to Goodbook. "What's the latest with the new casino? Where is Emdina? How do you spell that? Did I say it right?"

"Well, its spelled M-D-I-N-A but you said it right."

The waiter appeared at their side with the water. "Is everything alright gents?"

Goodbook put down his knife and fork, "It's better than alright mate, thank you. Listen do you know this place Mdina?"

"Aha," said the waiter, "the Silent City. In the middle ages it was the capital of Malta and it's a Citadela, or a citadel as you would say in English."

Door looked up at him. "What's a citadel?"

"It's a walled city. They built it on one of the highest points in Malta, better to defend the Maltese from invaders."

Goodbook interrupted the waiter. "That would be the people, not the candy." Door gave him a look and the waiter continued.

"Most of the walls are still intact and it's mostly a precinct, although residents are allowed to take their cars in. Streets are very narrow."

Door was impressed. "Wow, a walled city. And people live there. Is it far from here?"

The waiter smiled, "People do live there and there are restaurants and even a hotel inside the walls. It's about twenty minutes away, we say everywhere is ten minutes in Malta, but this is a little further."

"Mate, what's the easiest way to get there, a train, bus, get a cab maybe?" said Goodbook

The waiter seemed to find this amusing, as did the women on the next table who were now taking an interest in the conversation.

"There are no trains in Malta," said the waiter, smiling broadly, "and as for the buses, hmm, probably not. I think your best bet is to hire a car, they're cheap here and....."

Goodbook interrupted him. "But mate we don't know our way around to go driving about."

"It's okay," said the waiter, "Malta is only seventeen miles long by eight miles wide so it's quite difficult to get lost!" He turned and nodded to a young couple coming up the stairs to the restaurant.

"A hire car is your best bet. Excuse me please," he said, and left to attend to the arriving couple.

"He's right," said the tall woman at the next table, leaning towards them, "then you can go to Gozo as well." "Gozo?" said Door.

"You will have to excuse my friend here," Goodbook said, "he's geographically challenged, don't even know where Uzbekistan is!"

By the looks on their faces neither do they, thought Door.

Goodbook turned to face him. "Mate, there are two islands in Malta and Gozo is the other one. It's just up the road. There's a car ferry to take you over."

Another of the three women decided to chip in. "Ah, but did you know there's a time difference in Gozo?" she said, looking from one to the other. Her head moved from side to side, watching them intently, like a spectator at a tennis match. A little tipsy this one, thought Door.

"Like what, an hour forward?" he said.

"No!" she exclaimed, beaming, "twenty-five years back!" She fell about laughing and knocked over her wine glass." Door and Goodbook exchanged a look.

The taller one spoke again. "Also, if you hire a car you can go to Sicily," she said, pointing out to sea. The tipsy woman was nodding in agreement while the pretty one mopped up the wine spill with a paper napkin.

"It's only an hour on the Hydrofoil."

"Are there any casinos there?" asked Door.

"Don't think so," she replied. The women conferred for a moment.

"No, we don't think there are, but there are some here." She said something to her friends that Door could not understand, and they each nodded. Then they stood up, making ready to go. Door stood up as well.

"You're leaving so soon, you haven't eaten anything."

The pretty one answered him. "No, we only came for a drink. We're going to Parch Ville now to party on." She gave him a big smile. "Maybe you can join us later?"

Door grinned. "Well, maybe, yes perhaps we could do that. How do I find this place, is it close by?

The tall one answered him. "Just head up the hill and keep going. You will see a sign saying Paceville," she said, spelling it out for him.

"It's Malta's nightlife area. We say it Parchville and there are lots of bars, clubs and discos. If you fancy a drink you'll find us at Inertia, about half-way down the steps. But only if you come soon, we usually have a drink there and then move on to Feugo. We'll be in one of them, for sure. You'll find them easy enough."

"Okay," said Door, "thanks for the invite, we'll try and catch you guys later."

As they were leaving the tipsy woman leaned over and spoke to Goodbook.

"Actually, there are four," she said.

"Pardon me miss, four what?"

"Four islands in the Maltese archipelago, the others being Comino and Filfar."

She smiled and hurried to catch the other two who were already on the steps.

Door continued standing until they left, waving as they disappeared.

Goodbook poured more wine into their glasses and raised his.

"Cheers mate, here's to you, I think you may have pulled."

"Well, let's hope so. You up for a drink later with those girls?"

"Nah mate, I'm probably gonna turn in but I might stay here a little while longer and spend some time with me mate Jack."

"Daniels?"

"That's him! Actually, I could have got that for my new name, now you mention it."

"So, you're cool if I join up with them after we're done here?"

"No worries mate, you go and give the ferret a run!"

Door smiled. "Jules you are a star my man. Cheers," and he raised his glass.

"One thing though, can you tell me when this new casino is going to open?"

Goodbook frowned. "Well, the word is that the project's running late so it might be another three weeks before it opens, maybe a month." Door was bemused how his friend would get 'the word' here in this tiny European country where neither of them had been before.

"So, what do we do in the meantime?" he asked

"Mate, we do some tourist stuff, sightseeing and that, check out the Silent City, maybe go deep sea fishing."

"What about some diving?"

"For you that's a very real possibility, muff diving if I'm any judge! Anyway, we can just have a bit of a holiday for the next few weeks, take it easy. We had a good run up in Kopar and made some decent dosh so we can chill. Keep our powder dry, so to speak. But we could always," he left the sentence unfinished. "Always what?" said Door, puzzled.

"Mate, there are four casinos here already, so while we're waiting for the new place to open, we could give the blackjack a bashing. But on the level, no ace location or counting. You up for that?"

Door finished his wine and put the glass down. "That could work," he said, "so long as we don't fly above the radar and get on the local shit-list before the new place opens. Not be seen together of course, just play some basic strategy to see if that raises the alarm. I'll need to get some practice though, I'm a little rusty, haven't played blackjack in a long time, never mind chase aces."

"Too busy chasing arses," said Goodbook.

"Let me think about it," said Door. He stood up and tried to catch the eye of the waiter inside the restaurant.

"Don't worry about the bill mate," said Goodbook, emptying the last dregs of the wine out of the bottle into his glass.

"I'll sort it out. You get along after those Sheilas. Make your move before someone else does."

"Thanks Jules, think I will."

"No worries mate. But listen, before you go, I thought you were a bit slow tonight."

"What do you mean by slow?"

"You never introduced yourself to those girls like you normally do, that's not like you."

"Well, that's because of my identity crisis!"

"What identity crisis?"

"Well, in Malta is I Cliff Door or is I Frank Burt?" he said, using the same loud deep voice he used before.

"You have a point mate. Need to think that one through. If you see that lot later," said Goodbook, nodding at the table the girls had left, "what will you tell them?"

Door smiled at him as he turned to go down the steps to the street.

"I'm gonna tell them that I'm Frank and you're that dog."

"What dog?"

"Rin Tin Tin," he said, laughing out loud. "Don't wait up. Woof!"

CHAPTER ELEVEN

MALTA - PORTOMASO

Browning's taxi drew up at the Malta Hilton and he could see Meadows leaning on a railing, looking down over the adjacent marina. Browning thought he looked very relaxed, taking in the late afternoon sunshine, smoking a cigar. He paid the driver and gave his name and suitcase to the doorman before strolling over to join Meadows at the railing.

"Lovely spot this, impressive, don't you think?" said Meadows, waving his arm in a sweeping gesture over the small, U-shaped marina below them. A dozen or so power boats of varying sizes were moored stern-in to the quayside, gently bobbing and swaying in the afternoon breeze. On three sides of the marina, modern apartment blocks rose five stories while a variety of restaurants sat on the mezzanine level between the quays and the apartments. Diners on the terraces looked out over the main marina harbour and another smaller mooring area where sailing boats were berthed in the shelter of a breakwater, protecting them from the open sea beyond.

"Certainly looks a good spot," said Browning, "is this the project you're involved in?"

"No, I wish it had been. Mine is up the east coast, near Meliha. Not so grandiose as this." Meadows turned around and pointed at a tower building with a blue glass facade across from the Hilton driveway. "This project, Portomaso, has the marina, residential apartments, commercial outlets, restaurants, bars, a casino, that monstrous business tower and the Hilton all on the same footprint. It was developed a few years back on the site of the old Malta Hilton which sat on a cliff-top just about where we're standing." He leaned back on the railing, tilting his head back to view the top of the tower. "They moved millions of tons of earth and rock, dumping it out at sea, to bring the site down to sea-level to create this development. Some vision."

"Well, I have to say I'm impressed," said Browning. He pointed to a neon sign at the base of the tower that announced, The Casino. "There was a full-page ad for that casino in the in-flight magazine. And at the airport there were some huge signs advertising Dragonara Casino. How many casinos are there here?"

"Dragonara is the oldest, been around for decades and is owned now by local interests in partnership with a French casino group. Then the Maltese company that built Portomaso secured a casino licence and opened Oracle Casino in Bugibba, a touristy town up the coast. Later they opened The Casino here on the back of the Oracle's licence. Apart from those three, there's another casino on the other side of the Grand Harbour, Casino de Venicia, which is about half an hour's drive from here. It's owned in part by the Venetian Commune, or council, who own the casino on the Grand Canal in Venice. Local investors own the rest.

"Seems a lot of casinos for such a small place," said Browning.

Meadows smiled. "Five or maybe six families own pretty much the lion's share of everything in Malta and naturally there's a rivalry between them. One such family opens a casino, so another family wants one. They plead their case to the Minister responsible for gaming and he decides another licence is appropriate. And then, hey presto, another casino opens its doors."

Browning considered this for a moment. "So, does Grima belong to one of the premier families?"

"No, but he's a serious wannabe, striving to match their wealth and position." Meadows looked at his watch, "Doug why don't you check in and I'll meet you in the lounge by the lobby. Grima's driver will be here on the hour to take us for a meeting, so we have time for a coffee and a chat before we go."

Up in the room Browning's suitcase was waiting for him so he unpacked a few items, hung up a suit, and stepped out onto the balcony. Immediately below him was the hotel pool, complete with a sandy beach, set in colourful gardens of flowering bushes and swaying palm trees. Beyond them the deep-blue waters of the Mediterranean Sea sparkled in the afternoon sunshine. Away to his left a large imposing stone building with columned terraces and a sweeping staircase sat majestically on the end of a spit of land jutting out into the sea. A tacky neon sign on its roof proclaimed 'Casino' in huge red letters.

Grabbing his laptop case, he made his way down to the lobby and saw Meadows sitting on a sofa, next to a grand piano, pouring coffee from a silver pot. He looked up and smiled as Browning approached. "How's your room, everything alright?"

Browning sat on the sofa opposite him. "Yeah, pretty good

thanks. Nice hotel, modern, airy. Big room, sea view, I like it. Would that be the Dragonara Casino I could see from my room?"

Meadows nodded, pointing to a coffee pot and cupcakes set out on a tray. "It is. Help yourself."

They sat for a while, Meadows staring out to sea while Browning watched the people ebb and flow in the lobby, the revolving doors turning constantly.

Meadows turned back to face Browning.

"Now about Joe Grima. Apart from owning a few small hotels in Malta that I mentioned before, he's recently ventured into time-share and residential property developments which he funds through several other interests — restaurants, night-clubs, and a couple of the larger supermarkets on the island. He inherited the family business which consisted just of a small hotel on the Sliema waterfront, so he's grown it into a sizeable enterprise. Then he secured a casino licence for one of his hotels and that's where we come in."

"I was curious about that," said Browning, "a celebrated Atlantic City 'somebody' hooks up with a Malta 'nobody' to operate a casino. How did that come about?"

"We met at a time-share conference in New York. He was there to get a feel for the business and looking for investors. For my part I was interested to get some property development experience in Europe as I'd been thinking for a while to shift some of my asset base outside the US. So, I saw a hook-up with him as a sort of low-cost entry to learn the ropes which would also give me a man on the ground. Our man in Europe if you like." He glanced at his watch. "So, tell me Doug, how did it go in London with your guy, what's his name? Shaggy?"

Browning smiled at the way Meadows side-stepped explaining where the casino project fitted in to his overseas property expansion plans.

"Shruggy. Yes, he's happy to come over and will help me put together a management team if we need it, depending on what we already have as hired by Grima. He's after a reasonable two-year deal, decent flat and three or four trips back to the UK each year with some sort of performance bonus if the local regulations allow for management bonuses."

Meadows held out his hand in a stop gesture. "Doug, you'll have to work out all that stuff with Grima. You won't encounter any problems with whatever you propose, it's your call but you just need to run it by him, he needs to keep face, you know, be seen to make those decisions, for appearances sake."

"Okay, will do. I appreciate it's my call but I'm also conscious of the fact that under the Meadowlands management contract it's also your money that I'll be spending on people like Shruggy."

"It's all good," said Meadows, getting to his feet and looking over at the revolving doors at the entrance. "I'm glad your man is joining us. I think we should make a move, I guess Grima's driver will be here soon." Browning thought it strange that he only ever referred to Grima by his surname, never Joe.

Right on cue, Grima's driver walked into the lobby, 'entering from stage left' thought Browning, a short, portly man in an ill-fitting Chauffeur's uniform with a peaked cap tucked under his left arm. He saw Meadows and nodded in recognition before going back outside. They followed him and got into the waiting black BMW.

They drove along a narrow road with the sea on the left and high-rise apartments to the right. At street level Browning noticed an

Irish pub, several real estate agencies, a variety of restaurants, bars, more pubs, and some small hotels mixed in with both very old and very new-looking apartment buildings. A wide promenade ran the entire length of the seafront and throngs of people were strolling along in both directions, eating ice-creams, taking pictures, fending off street vendors, pushing kids in strollers, walking dogs. All being dodged by the inevitable joggers and an occasional cyclist.

"Popular spot," said Browning, "tell me driver, what's this place called please?"

The driver adjusted his internal mirror to allow eye contact with Browning, sitting in the back of the car with Meadows.

"Please call me Alfred sir. This is Tower Road sir, Sliema. But the Hilton is in St Julian's." He spoke English with a sing-song accent and was sweating profusely despite the Limo being air-conditioned. Browning picked him for about sixty years old and thought he sounded a bit like an Italian.

"Okay, thanks Alfred," said Browning, "and how far are we from Valetta?"

"Ah, Valetta, it's the capital. You'll see it across the water as we come to Sliema Harbour in a moment." The Mercedes turned off Tower Road and they wound their way down a wide road with famous brand-name shops on either side and then the harbour appeared below them. Browning could see the skyline of Valetta, behind huge battlement walls, on the far side of the water.

"Looks impressive Philip," he said, "is it?"

"Well, I must admit Valetta has a certain old world charm. The fortifications are impressive, and the roller-coaster narrow streets are amazing," said Meadows, "but I'm personally not so keen. The architecture's interesting but it's difficult to get around and the main street is all about shopping. It's crowded morning 'til night. And I mean crowded. Hustle bustle, non-stop."

They drew up outside an imposing modern apartment block which faced the harbour. The driver showed them into a showroom at street level and announced, "Mr Grima's offices gentlemen."

The showroom turned out to be the sales office for Grima's developments, with large, showcased models depicting residential complexes with pools. Meadows guided Browning over to the largest model in the centre of the room. "Doug this is the project I'm involved in with Grima. Up the coast from here. It's partly a time-share complex and partly residential with high entry-level prices on the residential side." He waved his arm around the showroom. "The pictures on the walls there are the interior impressions." Browning looked around the room, taking in the pictures and counting four model showcases in all. Two seating areas with leather Chesterfield sofas and wooden coffee tables were enhanced with extravagant flower arrangements on stone plinths. The aroma of fresh coffee permeated the room. At the rear of the showroom two women in matching red and white outfits sat behind desks on either side of an ornate door, both talking on phones.

The door opened and a short, thick-set man emerged. He walked directly over to Browning and held out his hand. "Hello Mr Browning. I am Joe Grima, welcome to Malta. Merhba."

"Pleased to meet you Mr Grima," said Browning. They shook hands, Browning feeling that Grima had a weak grip for such a big man.

"I would like to thank you for coming to Malta and taking on this project for us. "He smiled at Meadows, and they shook hands too. "Please come into my office," he said, waving them through.

The office was small with glass sliding doors leading onto an enclosed courtyard. Browning saw that the courtyard, like the office, was completely bare. No plants or artifacts of any kind outside, just a bare concrete yard. Inside Grima's office there were no pictures of loved ones or development projects, no framed certificates on the walls, no personal items. A solitary laptop sat on a small, plain desk in the middle of the room with three moulded black plastic chairs for company.

Grima motioned for them to sit. He sat back in his chair, hands behind his head, and gazed at the ceiling as he spoke. "I don't know how much Mr Meadows has told you Mr Browning," he said, continuing to look at the ceiling and not at either of his guests, "but this project is in a difficult moment. I had a General Manager here, a certain Lloyd Baker, and so far as I could tell he was on top of things. He oversaw the equipment purchasing, worked on the casino design with our architects, worked well with my marketing team et cetera (he pronounced it "et chetera" which Browning found amusing) and chose the slot machines et chetera, et chetera. And then," he paused before continuing, "he left. Without warning."

At this point he turned his gaze from the ceiling to Browning. "Do you know this man, Lloyd Baker?"

"Well sort of," said Browning. "I know people who worked with him, so I've met him with them a few times at the gaming show in London. Why do you ask?"

"He was recommended to me by some casino people in London, where I like to play sometimes. Just interested to know what you think of him."

"Can't really comment, hardly know the man." Browning shrugged. "Does it really matter now if he's gone?"

Grima returned his gaze to the ceiling. "I suppose you are right. This man Baker became involved with one of the female trainees, and next thing we know he's left the island with her. Left his wife behind, who is still here, living in the apartment I rented for him." He looked at Browning. "Are you married Mr Browning?"

Browning smiled at him. "No." The two men looked at each other with Browning wondering what was coming next. There was another lengthy silence.

Grima spoke first. "Mr Syd Cowper has been looking after the casino project since Baker left, I believe you know him quite well."

Browning had a flashback of pulling a drunk, barely conscious Syd Cowper out of a bathtub in Swaziland after going to his flat to see why he hadn't turned up for work at the Hippo Creek casino.

"Why yes," he said, with his best engaging smile. "I know Syd. Haven't seen him for years but we worked together in Africa. Good guy. Works hard, plays hard, loves the water."

"Well, that's good," said Grima, "because I personally recruited him from the Dragonara Casino where he was a floor manager. He was here before Baker and set up the training school and when Baker arrived it was agreed that he would be Baker's assistant. So, I am expecting that you will find a place for him in your management team. Yes?"

Browning smiled. "Syd is okay, and I'm sure we'll work something out."

Grima stared at him. "He has done a good job for us here Mr Browning, took over everything in Baker's absence. Please keep that in mind." He sat back in his chair and gazed at the ceiling again. "The remainder of the equipment we are waiting for will arrive tomorrow in containers from the UK and will need to be cleared through customs. We can expect it to be ready to be delivered to the casino site in a couple of days."

"Good," said Browning, "do you have a list handy?"

"Mr Cowper has all the documents at the training school, which is not far from here." He sat forward and looked at Browning. "I suggest we go there now, and you can meet up with Mr Cowper and see the training school?"

"Would you mind if I go there on my own?" said Browning

Grima looked at Meadows who shrugged his shoulders.

"Okay, Mr Browning," said Grima, "if you prefer. I will arrange for one of our sales team to take you there."

Browning smiled at them both. He looked at Meadows. "If that's okay with you Philip, I'll see you back at the hotel in an hour or so. Also, Mr Grima when can we go and see the casino, please? Would it be possible tomorrow perhaps?" Grima was still gazing at the ceiling. Browning looked up at it too, but could not see anything worth looking at or out of the ordinary. Just a plain old ceiling.

He glanced at Meadows who smiled back at him with the tiniest shake of his head.

"I'll send my driver for you in the morning at nine to take you to the Silent City," said Grima, still looking at the ceiling. "I'll meet you there."

CHAPTER TWELVE

MALTA – RABAT

The bright red tourist train wound its way around Rabat's narrow twisting streets in the mid-day sun, it's three open-air carriages empty except for Goodbook and Door. A sign on the locomotive proclaimed 'Muson River 1894'.

"Where's Muson River, Jules?"

"Sounds Canadian to me," said Goodbook, his hand held in a salute to shade his eyes from the sun. "Moose on River, that's how they talk. Drop words like the, if, and, is, to, but. They say sun bright today. We go hotel, have drink. Chop up their sentences they do, the Canucks."

"Say what? They do not."

"They do so. Met loads of 'em in Australia. They all talk like that."

The train came to a halt as the recorded commentary announced they were at the Casino Notabile.

"This is our stop mate," said Goodbook.

"Thank God for that," said Door, stumbling in his haste to leave the carriage. "You can keep your train and your tour of Rabat, what a crock!"

"Mate, just thought you might like a little diversion, see the old town, the church, the catacombs and all that. Didn't plan on it being so hot though."

They left the train and found themselves standing by an old, stone building decorated with intricate carvings and cornices.

"You sure this is it, Jules?" said Door, fanning himself with a map of Malta.

"Well, up there, look, carved into the stone it says Casino Notabile and Notabile is a Maltese word for Mdina. As we're on our way to find the new casino in Mdina I saw this place on the train map and thought we should check it out. But it don't look right, eh? It's too small, don't you think?"

On a triangular raised terrace at the front of the building an old man was leaning on a broom, smoking a cigarette.

Goodbook called out to him, "Excuse me mate, is this the new casino?"

"No," said the man, smiling and obviously very amused at the question. "This is Casino Notabile, a National Monument, ta."

"Some monument," whispered Door. "Looks like it's falling down to me!"

The man continued, "It was built a long time ago as a gentleman's club and, in those days, they called such places a casino. Now they will restore it to host small weddings, meetings, things like that."

Door spoke, "Well, do you know anything about a new casino opening in Mdina, you know, a gambling place?"

The man shook his head and leaned over the balustrade. "If you go up this road," he said, pointing behind them, "there is a gate to Mdina across from the petrol station. Just enter the city and ask someone in there."

Goodbook waved at the man. "Okay, thanks mate."

With the sweat pouring off them it took about ten minutes to wander back up the hill and find their way to the Mdina Gate. Strolling across the stone footbridge they entered the Silent City. The cobbled street offered a number of tourist attractions including a Natural History Museum, the Mdina Dungeons — displaying various forms of torture through the ages — several gift shops, ice cream vendors and a Mdina Glass Shop, with locally blown glass, jewellery, figurines and objet d'art.

Despite the heat the street was crowded with tourists. The two men tagged on to the back of a walking tour, the leader holding up a multi-coloured umbrella while speaking German in a high-pitched voice. After just two or three minutes they came across the Xara Palace Hotel, a two-story building with a stone facade of similar style to the Casino Notabile.

Out front, a leafy courtyard was adorned with colourful umbrellas, tables and chairs. On the far side the tables were laid for dining, with white linen tablecloths and napkins on the place settings, whilst on the near side the tables were adorned only with a drinks menu. They ditched the walking tour and sat at the nearest unlaid table. Door waved at a waitress who came over to them and placed a couple of beer mats on the glass tabletop.

"Hello gentlemen. What can I get for you?" she said, holding a tray in one hand and twirling a strand of hair with the other.

"Two large beers would be great thanks," said Door, smiling his best smile at her.

She smiled back. "Local or imported?"

"Yeah, we'll try the local stuff please," Goodbook replied. She scribbled on a pad and went into the hotel through a service door at the corner of the building. Door watched her until she disappeared.

"She's pretty eh, Jules?"

"Mate, they're all pretty to you. Talking of which, did you catch up with those girls we met at Peppino's the other night?"

"Certainly did."

"So? How'd it go?"

"Ah well, you know, okay I guess."

"No, I don't know, that's why I'm asking!"

"Well, I caught up with them at Hugo's and we had a few drinks. I paired up with the pretty one."

"Of course, you did," said Goodbook. "No surprise there, eh?"

Door continued, "And we had a few drinks and a chat."

"And then what?" said Goodbook. "You went back to her place to play hide the sausage?"

"Jules, you should know that gentlemen never talk about such things."

"And since when were you a gentleman?"

Door grinned at him. "Well anyway, her name's Elaine and I'm seeing her again tomorrow night. Well, that's to say Frank Burt is seeing her tomorrow. Listen Jules, do you have any idea yet when this casino's going to open?"

"Not sure mate, but I think a couple of weeks."

They sat for a few minutes, cooling off in the shade. When the waitress reappeared with their beers, Goodbook spoke to her, "Excuse me miss, but do you know anything about a casino opening here sometime soon?"

"Ah, yes I do," she said, smiling as she put their check on the table. "Casino Mdina. It's going to open in a couple of weeks. I've been interviewed for a job there."

Door gave her a twenty Euro note with the check. "Oh, that's nice, good luck with that. Can you tell us where it is please?"

"Yes of course. But it's not here in Mdina. It's in Rabat. Go back out of the city the way you came in, and it's just behind the petrol station, in the Hotel Domus. You'll find it okay." She put the change on the table and turned to go.

"Just a minute miss," said Door, "you forgot this." He stood up and handed her a five Euro note. "Thank you, sir," she said, smiling at him, "just call me if you want something else." Door remained standing, watching her as she walked away.

"Mate, sit down will you?" said Goodbook, holding up his glass of beer and peering intently at the liquid. "You're making me nervous with all this chatting up going on."

"I'm not chatting her up, just being friendly."

"Yeah, I saw that! A five Euro friendship tip for two beers. Anyway, best left alone if she's going to work there, at the casino."

"Yeah, I suppose. Something wrong with your beer?" said Door, sipping the froth of his own.

Goodbook continued looking at his upraised glass, "Well it's a bit cloudy mate. Yours okay?"

"Tastes so-so but its bloody cold!"

"Well, here's cheers then mate. To Frank and Renton and Casino Mdina".

They clinked glasses.

CHAPTER THIRTEEN

LONDON - SHEPHERDS MARKET

Shruggy and Browning were sitting at a window table in the Kings Arms.

"So Duggie, I'm curious. Who are we meeting for dinner?"

"Nina Meadows, she's Philip's niece. In town to audition for a part in some new musical in the West End. Philip asked me to catch up with her, you know, keep an eye."

Shruggy smiled "Okay, got it. We meeting her here?"

"No, at L'Autre, just up the road there," said Browning, pointing out the window. "But I wanted you and me to chat a bit first. She's also staying at the Hilton so it's a short walk and she's okay with that, meeting us there."

"What's she like?"

Browning frowned. "Well, I haven't actually met her, only know her by sight. Spoke with her for the first time on the phone today to set up dinner tonight."

Shruggy grinned. "So, this is a formal meeting then. Better be on me best behavior cos you're out to impress the lady."

"Am I?" said Browning, smiling. "If you say so Shruggy, no flies on you."

"S'obvious innit," he shrugged. "So, tell me about Malta."

"Well, the opening's planned for a couple of weeks so I need you to be there soon. Like now ideally."

Shruggy grinned and pulled his passport out of his pocket. "Had this on me for days in case you called me over there. I can leave tomorrow if you want, I'm all set."

"Ah that's great Shruggy," said Browning. "I'll try and get you on the Air Malta flight from Heathrow tomorrow evening." He checked his watch. "Syd Cowper has been holding the fort over there since Lloyd Baker did the runner and he's done a good job. Without having any equipment for the training school, he made up roulette and blackjack tables using blankets and trestle tables. Drew the layouts with tailor's chalk. Looked good too. The trainee croupiers are coming along, should be ready. Uniforms are in hand. You okay with him?"

"Sure," said Shruggy, with an emphatic nod.

"Good. He's relieved to be kept on by us and being your number two is a bonus for him. He was scared we wouldn't want him. With a Maltese wife and two kids his job options in Malta are limited." Browning paused as something caught his eye outside in the street. After a few moments he turned back to face Shruggy. "While I was there the bulk of the equipment arrived, playing cards from Fournier, chips from Abbiati, gaming tables from TCS. Should be cleared through customs by now. Only thing we're waiting for is the roulette wheels. The slots are already on site, though still unpacked."

"Fournier cards is good news," said Shruggy, "but chips from that Italian lot. I didn't even know they made chips."

"Well actually I'm not sure the chip order is big enough. You'll need to review it and decide if we need more. Probably won't get any more in time for the opening, so you'll have to consider that when you set the table floats."

"So how many tables?" said Shruggy.

Browning sipped at his orange juice. "Four American roulettes, six blackjack, a Caribbean Stud and two Punto tables, one stand-up and one sit-down."

"A sit-down Punto Banco?" said Shruggy. " I haven't seen one of those in years."

"Nor me," said Browning, "not sure if there's a market for it these days. But we'll run with it to begin with anyway, like a novelty game perhaps. There's also 80 slots and a second-hand Royal Ascot horse racing machine that Grima picked up in an arcade in Belgium. I'm not so sure there's a market for that either, it's a bit old hat really. But Grima thinks it will do well as they have one at Oracle Casino."

"So Grima's a punter then," said Shruggy.

"Why do you say that?"

"Well, s'obvious innit, a sit-down Punto and a Royal Ascot. Only a punter would see any value in them." He shrugged.

Browning considered this for a moment. "Yeah, you're right Shruggy. He does like a punt. You always had a nose for these things. You know a slots guy called Van der Heyden? "

"Jan Van der Heyden?"

"That's him. Apparently, he worked at The Carousel, but I don't remember him. Is he any good?" said Browning, returning his gaze to the street.

Shruggy nodded, "Yeah, 'Jan Van' we called him." He was at The

Carousel when I was there. I didn't have much to do with the slots team generally, you know how they are, but he was alright. South African bloke. Pretoria was actually his home town. Took me to play golf out there. Very helpful and a good people person. A spunk of a sister he has too. He came over from Sun City after you went to Aruba. He's in the team?"

Browning nodded again. "He is. Slots manager. Grima pinched him from Dragonara where he was just a shift manager, so this is a step up for him. It's good you're okay with him as I couldn't get anyone from the Oceanic."

He pointed outside. "Your car jockey friends are outside. The ones we saw last time we were here."

Shruggy leaned over to the table to view the street. "So they are. Having a smoke I suppose." He shrugged.

Browning turned back from the window. "You haven't asked me about your deal?"

Shruggy smiled at him. "Doug, I know whatever you got me it's the best I could get. S'obvious innit. I'm happy just to be working with you again. But I was thinking. Do I need a Maltese gaming licence? Cos they can take ages to be issued, as you know well enough."

"You do," said Browning, looking at his watch again, "and so do I. But we'll work with temporary licences for the time being. Given that the operation was in danger of falling apart, the Maltese gaming authority have been very co-operative in that respect."

He stood up from the table. "We have to go Shruggy, Nina will be on her way to the restaurant."

Stepping outside they were approached by the two car jockeys. The shorter one of the two stood in front of Browning, blocking his path.

"You're Browning, aren't you?" he said. "Do you know who I am?"

Browning could smell alcohol on the man's breath. "No I don't," he said, "but you look vaguely familiar. Don't think I ever worked with you though."

The man stepped closer to Browning. "No, but you worked with my brother, Noel Gaston. At the Stanhope. Remember him?"

"Ah yes, now I do," said Browning, "the punchy cockney with a French name. You look a bit like him. How's he doing?"

"Not so good. He's driving a mini cab you prick, cos you got him fired. Lost his gaming licence. Now he can't get work in casinos anymore."

"Well, that's what happens when you punch someone out for no reason. Still punchy is he, your brother, still picking on people half his size? Or has he grown out of it?" He smiled at Gaston.

Gaston raised his fists level with Browning's face. "You arrogant cunt, I'll give you something to grow..." Browning's left fist slammed into Gaston's throat, and he dropped to the pavement, eyes bulging, gasping for breath.

The other car jockey, the tall one that Shruggy knew, lifted his hands, palms open in a defensive gesture as Browning turned on him, fists raised in a boxer's stance. The man backed away. "This ain't my fight," he said.

Browning dropped his hands and nodded at him.

"Let's go Shruggy," he said. Licking his left hand, he strode away without looking back at Gaston who was writhing on the pavement, clutching his throat.

CHAPTER FOURTEEN

LONDON - L'AUTRE

Shruggy stood for a moment looking down at the distressed figure of Gaston on the pavement and then set off after Browning, having trouble catching up with him. Within a few moments they reached L'Autre, it's bow fronted window glowing like a beacon of hope and hospitality in the gloomy, dank evening air. Two red shaded table lamps shone on the window sill inside where several red glass T-light holders glimmered and twinkled, jostling for space with a dozen dusty red wine bottles scattered haphazardly on the sill. A sign on the wall above the window proclaimed 'Polish-Mexican Bistro' and a wooden shield attached to the wall by the front door boasted 'Mayfair's Oldest Wine Lodge'.

Shruggy leaned on Browning for support by the door to the restaurant, catching his breath. "I must have passed this place a million times, but I never really noticed it until now," he said, puffing away, raising his eyebrows.

"You been here before Doug?"

Browning nodded, pausing for a moment to look back the way they had come, before leading Shruggy into the restaurant.

The interior was reminiscent of old English pubs with exposed beams, traditional dark wood tables and chairs. It was a small room, dominated by an imposing bar counter that was laden with yet more dusty red wine bottles and a straw sombrero perched on a block of wood. The bar's back wall featured two rows of spirit bottles with well-known and obscure brands standing side by side. Bank notes from dozens of countries were pinned to the front of the shelves. Perched on top of the unit were two blackboards advertising, respectively, the wine specials and imported beers, whilst a third said the food specials were Golonka and Bigos or Mexican Lamb Shank.

Shruggy noticed that while the wine bottles on the window sill and bar counter were dusty there was not a speck of dust to be seen anywhere else. Browning spoke briefly with the man behind the bar and turned back to face Shruggy. At that moment the front door opened and in walked Nina Meadows. She stood close to Shruggy and he, the former earth-bound hawk, immediately took in her blue eyes behind over-long eyelashes, shimmering red hair falling onto her shoulders, aquiline nose and a Miss World figure packed into five-feet-two. "Crikey," he thought. "A real beauty. Who is this?"

She looked past Shruggy to Browning and smiled. "Hello Douglas, we meet at last," she said, offering up her right hand for a handshake. Shruggy melted as she edged past him. Browning put his hands on her shoulders and kissed her on the cheek. She blushed.

"Hey Nina, nice to finally meet you too. Welcome to London and

L'Autre." He removed his right hand from her shoulder and placed it on Shruggy's shoulder. "And this is my longtime friend Raymond."

Shruggy offered his right hand, and they shook. "Hello Nina, call me Ray. How's it going?"

"Yes good, thank you Ray," she said, her voice wavering, "nice to meet you too."

Browning led them to a small corner table next to a fireplace, it's mantlepiece adorned with more dusty wine bottles whilst above them a huge ornate gilt-edged mirror was bedecked with fairy lights. Nina took the bench seat by the wall and the two men sat in wooden armchairs.

"It's a bit of a squeeze, eh," said Browning as he sat down, " but I'm sure we'll manage okay." He smiled at Nina. "Is this alright for you Nina? You ever had Polish food?"

"Don't think so, but I'm up for it. Try something new. Works for me," she said, smiling at him.

"Well, they also have Mexican food," Browning said. "What about you Shruggy, you up for it? Or you gonna have Mexican?"

"Shruggy?" said Nina, before Shruggy could answer, tilting her head to one side, smiling at him with her best smile.

Shruggy responded with his own number one smile. "Well yes, my surname is Shoulders, so everyone calls me Shruggy. S'obvious innit." He shrugged. Nina put her hand to her mouth to cover her giggles.

He looked at Browning and back to Nina. "Something funny?"

"I'm sorry," she said, still giggling, "that's just so weird. Shruggy Shoulders."

"Weird? Don't see it," said Shruggy, and he shrugged. She laughed out loud.

The waiter appeared with the menus and said, "Can I get you

something from the bar, an aperitif or a cocktail perhaps?"

They ordered a beer for Shruggy, a bourbon over ice for Nina and orange juice for Browning.

"Douglas," said Nina, "do you know your hand is bleeding?" pointing at his left hand. The knuckles were grazed, and a little blood seeped from the wounds. She reached into her handbag and offered him a tissue.

"Thanks Nina, sorry about that, scraped my hand opening the door." He said, smiling at her as he dabbed the tissue on his hand.

The drinks arrived and Shruggy held up his glass. "Cheers," he said, "and welcome to London, Nina".

"Cheers," she said, taking a big pull at the bourbon." Douglas, it's so very nice to meet you." Browning did not respond, just looked at her. "Don't you don't drink?" she asked him.

"Not so much," he replied, "used to, but not lately though. So, tell us about your trip here. Philip said you have an audition for a show. Is that right?"

"Yes, it is. They're casting for a new musical, don't know the name yet, it's a secret. But my agent says the production company is sound, he's dealt with them before, and he thinks it's worth a shot." She twirled a strand of hair as she talked. "But I've only ever sung in Atlantic City, you know, casino lounges, so this is a big step." She smiled at them both and took another sip at the bourbon. "I'm quite nervous about it all. The audition, being in a show and living in London if I get the part."

"Well, if you sound as good as you look, I'm sure you'll breeze it," Shruggy said.

Nina blushed. "Why thank you Shruggy," she said, raising her glass to him with a beaming smile. Now Shruggy blushed.

"Okay, I'm going to have the lamb shank special," Browning said. He put the menu down and looked at the others. "Have you decided?"

Yeah, lamb shank for me," chirped Shruggy, and took a long pull at his beer.

Nina fidgeted with the menu. After a while she looked at Browning and said, "Douglas, I need to go to the powder room. Will you order for me please? I just don't know what I fancy. But I eat everything so anything you choose will be just fine." Both men stood as she rose from the table, which seemed to amuse her. They watched her until she was out of sight, Shruggy wondering how she managed to get into those jeans, they were so tight.

He leaned close to Browning. "What was all that about back there Doug? Geez you flattened that bloke Gaston."

Browning dabbed at his grazed knuckles with the tissue. "Yeah, sorry about that Shruggy, you know these people. You can't reason with them. It was more out of anger at his brother, George, prick he was. He broke the jaw of some Spanish boy working in the kitchens at the Stanhope. This was just after you left to go to open The Carousel. The kid changed the TV channel in the staff room when George went to get a cup of coffee. When George returns, a sizeable bloke he is, he just goes over and punches the kid in the face. No warning, no argument, no nothing. Just punched his lights out. CCTV got him cold. It was on my shift, so I suspended him. Sent the report to my director and someone in human resources decided he had to go. Not me. But obviously I got the blame."

Shruggy finished his glass of beer and turned to signal the waiter to come over. He looked back at Browning. "Okay, I get all that. But geez you moved so quick. Where'd you learn all that stuff? Couldn't you have just walked away?" he said, leaning close to Browning, waiting for an answer. But Browning remained silent.

The waiter arrived and Browning ordered three lamb shanks and Shruggy asked for another beer. When he'd gone Shruggy sat back in his chair.

"Moving on then," he said, smiling, "your Nina is some looker."

"My Nina?" Browning replied, his eyebrows raised.

"Well, s'obvious innit? It's like static electricity between you two. You touch her and there'll be a spark! And, my god, she looks like Sandy. Apart from her hair. Dontcha think?"

Browning frowned at him. Nina returned to the table and they both stood up for her.

"My oh my," she said, assuming a deep south accent, "I feel like royalty at this table."

"Gentlemen always stand for a lady at table," Shruggy said. "S'obvious innit, but you're not used to it eh."

"I'm not," she said, "but I can get used to it." She looked at Browning. "So, Douglas I hear you're going to Malta to open a casino for Philip."

Browning smiled at her. "I am, and so is Shruggy. In fact, he's going tomorrow."

"Yeah," Shruggy said, "I'll do all the work and Doug will get all the credit. That's how it works. S'obvious innit?" He smiled at them both, pleased with his précis of the situation.

In return Browning and Nina smiled at each other as if Shruggy wasn't there. He shrugged and sat back in his chair, as if to distance himself from the magnetism he could feel, almost touch, building between them. Sandy all over again.

CHAPTER FIFTEEN.

SWAZILAND - HIPPO CREEK HOTEL CASINO - EIGHT YEARS EARLIER.

As Shruggy pulled up outside the hotel in the late afternoon, Browning was waiting for him.

"Hey Shruggy, you finally made it. I was expecting you hours ago."

Shruggy stepped out of his car, stretching, and groaning.

"Boy it's hot ain't it?" he said, grabbing Browning's outstretched hand. "Took me six fucking hours. Dirt roads some of it, car's full of dust, my hair's full of dust, my mouth's like the floor of a hyena's cage. They need to build that fucking airport at Manzini. S'obvious innit. Six bloody hours driving from Pretoria. Must be mad." He grabbed an overnight bag from the boot and tossed the car keys to the hovering doorman, a turbaned smiling man resplendent in a military style uniform. "And what's he so happy about?"

Browning put his arm around his friend. "Okay mate, I see you're tired and cranky, fair enough. Let's just go inside and get a drink and shake the journey off."

They walked through the lobby and into the casino where Browning ushered Shruggy to the bar. They leaned on the counter and Browning ordered two beers. The serving girl smiled at him and moved backwards away from them.

"I'm so glad you came mate," said Browning, "I've been here about a month now, and it's good to see a friendly face."

"Natives not friendly then?" said Shruggy, looking around the empty casino.

"No, you know how it is, new kid in town and all that. The General Manager I took over from was here for perhaps ten years or more. Franco Ricci, you know him?"

Shruggy shook his head. The serving girl arrived with the beers, and having placed them carefully on beer mats, smiled at the two men and backed away again. "What's that all about," said Shruggy, "the walking backwards thing?"

"The King of Swaziland traditionally has several wives, I dunno, seven or eight, and they have to walk behind him at all times. Act subservient, be submissive, all that stuff. So, it comes from that I guess."

"What?" said Shruggy, slapping Browning on the shoulder. "So now you're like a king down here?"

Browning smiled. "No, of course not. King Dick more like, but the locals are inclined to back away from people in authority. The King has so many children probably half the staff here are royalty. This girl is likely a princess"

Shruggy picked up his beer. "You're kidding."

"Absolutely not," said Browning, grinning. "Cheers mate."

They clinked glasses and pulled at the beers, Shruggy downing half of his in one go. Browning gestured to the serving girl to bring two more beers.

"I have to say Shruggy, you're looking good, still working out?" he said.

"Yeah, not much else on the go in Pretoria so my routine is work, gym, pub. But never mind all that, what's the drill?" asked Shruggy, "what's the plan for my visit? You didn't ask me down here just so we could get pissed together." Browning smiled. Shruggy continued, "I figure you want me to take a look at this flea-pit you're running and tell you what I think. S'obvious innit?"

He shrugged and finished the rest of his beer.

Browning waved his hand across the lifeless casino. "Yeah, something like that. This place is old and not just a little tired, needs a major refurb. Most of the slots are out of date. I've got just two surveillance guys who double as security, they're only here at peak times, but as you can see mid-week is dead. We only run the table games during the day at weekends and holidays, but I keep the bar and coffee shop open to support what little slot action we have."

He paused as the second round of beers arrived and waited until the serving girl backed away before continuing "The CCTV system itself is okay, but the camera locations need re-working, stuff like that. But I can sort all that. I'm more concerned about building up the business, because to be honest Shruggy I don't know how long I will stay here if I can't add some value. I know the Carousel is honking so I'm interested to see if there's anything you guys are doing there, you know, marketing, high rollers, in-house promotions that I could use here."

Shruggy smiled at him, more relaxed now the alcohol was having some effect.

"Okay Doug, I figured that's what it was. Plus, you've got with-drawal symptoms from not having seen me for so long. Anyway, I have some ideas for you, s'obvious innit, but tomorrow, eh. I'm bushed now."

"Of course. Tomorrow will be just fine," said Browning, "I've got other plans for us right now. You go and freshen up and I'll meet you in the lobby in half an hour cos I'm going to take you into Siteki for dinner."

"Siteki?"

"It's a one-horse town without a horse, just up the road from here. We have some staff accommodation there. And there's a great steak house with a terrific wine list, mostly South African wines of course, but streets ahead of anything we have here."

They returned to the lobby where Shruggy picked up his room key from reception. "I'll just dump my bag and I'll see you soon," he said and followed the ever-smiling doorman down the corridor to his room.

As Browning headed off to his office the girl on reception called out to him. "Mr Douglas sir, there is a lady here to see you please."

Browning returned to the counter. "To see me?" he said.

"Yes, Mr Douglas sir. She is sitting over there waiting for you," she said, pointing across the lobby.

Browning turned and saw a very attractive, well dressed young woman sitting by the window. Her blonde hair shone in the after-noon sunlight.

She smiled and stood as he approached her.

"Mr Browning? I'm Sandy," she said, holding out a gloved hand.

Now who is this, he wondered, dressed for Hollywood and look-ing like a million dollars, out here in the back arse of nowhere.

He took hold of her hand, gently, as if his grasp might somehow damage it.

"Hello Sandy. It's a pleasure to meet you. But I don't know why you're here or why you're waiting for me."

"Oh sorry. My name is Cassandra Waring," she blushed.

Browning realised he was still holding her hand and reluctantly let go.

"Ah yes, Cassandra, now I've got you. You're the croupier hired by Signor Ricci. I was expecting you to arrive tomorrow. No?"

She blushed again, "Yes that's right, but my mate who drove me down here from Joburg could only do it today. I hope that's okay?"

Browning smiled his best smile, "Well yes, of course. But we'll have to find a room here for you tonight as your staff accommodation in Siteki won't be ready until tomorrow."

"Oh, I hope that's okay, I'm really sorry."

"No problem. Can I offer you a drink at the bar?"

"That would be nice, I could murder a coldie after that drive."

He led her towards the casino bar. "Which part of Australia are you from?"

She blushed once more. "How did you know that? Oh, I suppose you read it in my application form," she smiled. Browning thought she had the whitest teeth he'd ever seen.

"Well actually no," he said. "I haven't read your file yet, but I have heard an Australian accent before." He smiled at her. "Also, coldie is a bit of a giveaway." She nodded and grinned and then they stood for a moment, smiling at each other.

Browning was amazed that she looked so cool and relaxed in comparison to Shruggy's appearance and demeanor upon his arrival, given they had both made almost the same journey.

They moved up to the bar and sat on high stools facing each other. Browning ordered two beers.

"I'm from Hobart, Tasmania," said Sandy.

"Aha, so you trained at Wrest Point Casino?"

"Spot on. Blackjack, roulette, punto, you know. Then got the wanderlust and here I am."

"And why Sandy? Not Cassandra, or Cass?"

"At school they nicknamed me Big Bird, after a cassowary. Like a twist on my real name, and I hated it. Great big gangly thing, a cassowary is. So, I chose Sandy. Plus, I have this of course," she said, smiling as she twirled a lock of her blonde hair.

The beers arrived and they raised glasses.

"Sandy it is then," said Browning, with a broad smile

"Thank you Mr Browning," she said, with a smile that topped his.

"Please call me Douglas."

She took a big pull at the beer. "Cheers then Douglas, it's so very nice to meet you."

CHAPTER SIXTEEN

LONDON - HILTON ON PARK LANE

Browning awoke to the sound of rain hammering on the windows. Swinging his legs around slowly he stepped out of the bed, not wishing to wake Nina as she lay asleep in a foetal curve, snoring softly. He went to the bathroom and grabbed a toweling robe, throwing it on as he moved over to the window. Lightning flashed in the distance and for a second London's skyline was swathed in an eerie, white shroud. Then darkness again as the city slept, the lights from street lamps, neon signs, floodlit buildings and monuments flowing into each other in kaleidoscopic rivulets on the pane of glass. He went to the mini-bar and emptied a miniature bottle of Jack Daniels into a tumbler.

Returning to the window the dream that disturbed his sleep came back to torment him. Sandy was sitting on a wall, in bright sunlight, smiling and calling to him. But as he tried to go to her, she faded away, faded into nothing. Just her voice remained, calling him. He drank some of the bourbon and began to cry.

A massive thunderclap exploded overhead, the lightning strike so devastatingly bright it blinded him. He reeled away from the window, the drink sloshing over his hand.

Nina woke up and turned on the bedside lamp, struggling to sit up whilst at the same time trying to cover herself with the duvet. Browning moved over and sat on the edge of the bed next to her, licking the bourbon off his hand. He mused how strange it was that women do that, cover their nakedness before a man they have just had sex with. "You okay?" he asked.

"Ah, I guess so," she replied, fussing first with her hair and then the covers.

She pointed at the tumbler. "I thought you didn't drink."

"I haven't been. For quite a while."

"But you are now?"

He nodded. "Seems like."

She leaned towards him and held his chin gently, turning his face towards hers. "Is it because of me?" She smiled. "Don't tell me I've driven you to drink?"

He tried to return the smile, but it wouldn't come. "No, it's not you. Well, in a way it's about you. It's difficult to explain." He wiped away a tear.

Nina leaned closer again and, seeing his tears, put an arm round his shoulders. "Well, first you can pour me some wine and then you can explain. Tell me about it. We have all night."

And so it was. Browning began to speak, slowly at first, choosing his words carefully before everything just flooded out. A pent-up torrent of emotions bursting the banks of his secret river of pain. About how Nina evoked memories of a lost love called Sandy. About their instant, passionate attraction when they met in Africa, their binge drinking, their boozy picnic trip up-country in a mini moke, the tornado roaring out of nowhere, crashing through the scrub and hitting them side-on.

Sandy's scream as the wind tore her from her seat, his howling as he lost control of the moke in his drunken daze, rolling it, being knocked unconscious. Only to wake up battered, bruised, bleeding and Sandy gone. Vanished. Never to be found. Ever.

The local villagers who came to his aid believed that hyenas took her, or she ended up in the river where crocodiles or the currents finished her. The images tortured him, not knowing haunted him. The guilt almost killed him. Friends told him it wasn't his fault, nothing he could have done, but it was his nemesis.

The horror crippled him and since that day he'd not touched alcohol and refused to drive.

He flew to Hobart with Sandy's clothes and personal effects to give them to her parents, thinking it would be the right thing to do. It wasn't. Her father was inconsolably grief-stricken, catatonic almost, and her mother gave him the Medusa stare, turn you to stone.

He jobbed around Australia for a year, deckhand on a clapped-out, leaking, deep-sea prawn trawler, picking fruit in the river-lands, mending fences on a sheep station, volunteering at a hospital by day and cashiering in a petrol station at night, keeping busy to blind-side reality and find some peace, but failing.

Relating his macabre narrative left Browning utterly drained. He sank into a shallow, uneasy sleep in Nina's arms. Outside the thunderstorm abated, revealing the first glimmer of a watery dawn struggling to begin a new day.

CHAPTER SEVENTEEN

MALTA - THE STRAND, SLIEMA.

Goodbook checked his watch. Another ten minutes to go before meeting up with Door to catch the ferry across the harbour to have lunch in Valetta. He stood still, taking in the view of the Valetta battlements over the water.

"Excuse me sir," said a female voice behind him, "would you mind to take a photo for me please?" He turned around to see a tall, very attractive woman, in her forties he reckoned, decked out in designer casuals and reflective sunglasses, holding out her mobile phone.

He smiled. "Well, I'm a bit clumsy with these things," he said, taking the phone from her, "but I'll give it a go and try not to drop it!" He backed away a couple of feet.

"Do you want mostly you, or mostly the harbour?" he asked.

"Well, it is some sight to see, but if you can get me in the shot that would be really neat." She laughed and removed her sunglasses, smiling at him.

Goodbook pressed the phone and it clicked rapidly several times before he took his finger off the button. "Ah sorry about that, seems you have plenty of snaps to pick from."

He smiled as he gave the phone back. "Are you an American perhaps?"

"Canadian I am, but spent some time in the US. People often think I'm a yank."

"Ouch!" said Goodbook, screwing up his face. "Didn't mean to offend you."

She smiled at him for a moment. "Not offended. And you?" She stroked her chin with her index finger and thumb. "An Aussie I reckon."

Goodbook pulled a face. "Sprung. Once a Shackle-dragger always a Shackle-dragger. I guess it's obvious, eh?"

"Shackle-dragger?"

"You know, convicts, ball and chain." He mimicked dragging a chain, hauling one heavy foot to the other, then tiny steps before bringing the feet together again.

She laughed. "Shackle-dragger indeed."

He thought she had beautiful hair, so dark and shiny.

"Renton," he said, offering his hand. "Being the shy retiring type that I am, may I invite you to join me to imbibe some coffee, or even for tasting a glass of the local Maltese wine perhaps? I'm told it's sensational. If it's not too early in the day. And if I'm not being too forward. Even for an Aussie!"

She took his hand and shook it. Goodbook was surprised how firm her grip was. "Charmaine." She glanced at her watch and grinned at him.

"Why not?" she said. "I'm okay for time."

CHAPTER EIGHTEEN

MALTA - SLIEMA WATERFRONT.

Goodbook sauntered along the esplanade whistling Waltzing Matilda and smiled at Door who was waiting for him by the Sliema Ferry dock. Door did not smile back.

"Where the fuck have you been?" he said, pointing at his watch. "You're thirty minutes late. We'll lose the table at Cockneys, it's very popular."

"Don't fret mate, it's all good. My mate Abraham will make sure they keep the booking for us". He held up a US$5 note, Lincoln's stern face frowning at them as Goodbook scrunched the note in his fingers.

"Anyhow they serve lunch all day out here so if it's an issue we'll just have a drink at the bar until there's a table." He wrapped an arm around his friend and held him close. "No worries, Cliff my boy!"

Door twisted out of the hug and moved away. "Yeah, okay Jules, I guess you're right. Standing out here in the sun I got a little cranky."

He made a point of consulting his watch again. "The ferry's here, let's go."

The ferry's hull was painted an insipid shade of pale green with the word 'Lowenbrau' emblazoned in big black letters along the sides. They jostled with a group of camera wielding Japanese tourists to secure a bench seat in the front row of the bow section.

As the ferry left the dock, Door stood up and took three or four pictures with his phone but quickly sat down again. He steadied himself with his hand on Goodbook's shoulder. "I'm not good on boats," he said.

Goodbook sniffed. "Mate it's only a five-minute crossing, we're halfway already."

"That's funny, I thought Valetta Harbour was massive," said Door, looking around, his hand shading his eyes from the sun.

"It is mate, but it's on the other side of the city," said Goodbook, pointing over the massive battlements that towered over the shoreline. "This is Marsamxett Harbour, or Sliema Harbour if you prefer." He beamed at Door, pleased to show off his local knowledge. Door shrugged.

Leaving the ferry, they walked a short distance to the restaurant where a well-dressed waiter, who introduced himself as Angelo, welcomed them and led the way to the table reserved for Mr Tinn.

Angelo fussed and flurried with the menus and glasses of water, reeling off the lunchtime specials before prancing back to the entrance to welcome more new customers. "Threw me a bit he did," said Door, "when he called you Mr Tinn."

"Be good if you can remember who we are now, Frank," said Goodbook. "I told you it wouldn't be a problem with the table. Being late is a national pastime in Malta."

They studied the menu. "Jules I really like the feel of this place, it's airy, breezy, you know? I love this alfresco dining thing. Gonna have tuna carpaccio and the prawn dish he recommended on the specials."

"All good mate, I'll have the same. And a big beer. Not local, Heineken or something. Can you order it cos I need the boy's room?"

When he returned, he found Door standing up and chatting to two middle-aged women on the next table. "Ah yes," said Door to the women and extending his arm to Goodbook, "this is my good friend I was telling you about, the famous travel writer, Renton Tinn."

Goodbook nodded at them. Could be sisters maybe. "Ladies, are you enjoying Malta?" he said, stroking his chin. Charm personified.

The nearest woman, in a blue top, said, "Should be. Been living here for fifteen bloody years!" Goodbook thought she sounded Scottish.

The other one, in a red top, said, "Even me. But only been here ten." She smiled at Goodbook. "And you, do you like it? Frank said you're here doing a story for the New York Times. How exciting! Is it a love story perhaps?"

English this one, thought Goodbook, glaring at Door who was grinning at him over his glass of wine. "Well, more of a travelogue than a story, really," he said.

He sat down with a sigh of relief as Angelo returned with their carpaccio. Door continued exchanging pleasantries with the women for a moment before taking his seat.

Goodbook leaned over and spoke in a whisper, close to Door's face. "What the fuck was all that about? Remember, low profile, fly below the radar, don't draw attention to yourself."

"Jules, sorry, Renton. Just a bit of fun. Saw these old biddies and thought of you."

"Of me?"

"Yeah. The one in the red's not bad looking, about your age, thought I'd help you out." He grinned at Goodbook. "You know, a good turn, help you give the ferret a run."

"Mate, I'll have you know I don't need any help. Thank you. And by the way I have already met a lovely lady and we are going to dinner tomorrow. So, thank your mother for the rabbits."

"Hallelujah! There's hope for us all," said Door, raising his wine. "Cheers!"

Goodbook half-heartedly raised his beer. "You can take the piss mate, but this is a very nice woman, Canadian, and a good looker too."

"Canadian," said Door. "She from Muson River? She say, 'you me go out, no stay home eh'. "

Goodbook rolled his eyes to the heavens "Yeah alright smart arse. Anyhow, enough about me. Let's get up to date with you and TPO."

Door sat back in his chair. "TPO?"

"Yeah. TPO. The Pretty One. Elaine? The one you were sniffing around at Peppino's and with whom, if I'm not mistaken, you have been spearing the bearded clam." He opened his palms towards Door. "Have you not?"

Door responded by waving at Angelo and pointing to his empty wine glass.

"You've got this one right Jules. Elaine it is. Elaine Grima and she is terrific. Sexy as. She's married to some wealthy local property developer, but I gather there's not much between them. He's a lot older than her and busy, busy, busy. You know how it goes."

Now it was Goodbook's turn to catch Angelo's eye and signal for another beer.

"Yeah, I know how it goes alright. Just be careful, Cliff my boy, eh, low profile and all that. Malta's a small place and everyone knows everyone's business. We don't need some rich local bloke tell his goons to come looking for you cos you're at it with his missus."

CHAPTER NINETEEN

MALTA - VALETTA WATERFRONT.

L eaving Cockneys after their lunch, with smiley bye byes to the two women and a generous tip for Angelo, Goodbook and Door strolled down Boat Street towards the waterfront.

"Lovely meal that mate," said Goodbook, puffing on a cheroot.

"Yeah, it was good," said Door, looking around in all directions.

Goodbook stopped walking and confronted his friend. "Cliff my boy, what's the matter with you today? You're up and down like a lift driver's arse. You were touchy coming over here, chirpy at lunch and now you're all on edge. What's up?"

"Sorry Jules, I don't know. Just a sense of foreboding I guess."

"Foreboding. What the fuck is that?"

Door shrugged his shoulders. "Dont know. Just uneasy. Woke up with it."

"Woke up with a hangover more like. You on the piss last night, you and TPO?"

"No. Not really. No more than usual." He smiled at Goodbook. "Sorry mate, but look, I'll shake it off. And here's the ferry now."

They walked on, quickening their stride and making it to the dock as the last arriving passengers disembarked. There were already several people waiting to board so they waited patiently, becoming the last to embark. Goodbook acknowledged a no-smoking sign and threw his cheroot into the water. He turned back to speak to Door, but he was gone. Nowhere to be seen.

He looked over at the dock, but Door was not there, so he went back to the stern but there was still no sign of him. The ferry pulled away from the shore and he walked back to the bow section and there, struggling to hold onto a flapping tourist map, was Charmaine.

"Well, well, well, knock me down with a feather," he said, giving her his best smile. "Fancy meeting you here. That's twice in one day. It's a sign."

She laughed, " Well hi Renton. Don't know about a sign, Malta's a small place. But it's good to see you just the same." She finally managed to fold the map and put it into her handbag.

"Just had a look around St Paul's Cathedral in Valetta," she said, pointing at an imposing dome on the skyline as the ferry pulled away from the shore. "Have you ever been there?"

"Nah," he said, "churches and stuff not really my go. Had lunch at Cockney's with my mate that I told you about." He looked around, checking the other passengers to see if he could spot him. "I would like to have introduced you, but I don't know where he's got to. Vanished he has."

"Well, it's not a very big boat, he can't be far away."

"Yeah, actually he's not a very good sailor, maybe he's gone to the loo."

Charmaine took out her phone and took pictures of the Valetta skyline while Goodbook continued to look out for Door. As the ferry approached the Sliema dock she put her phone away and turned to Goodbook. "I'm sure you will find your friend, but I have to run so perhaps I'll meet him some other time," she said, offering her hand to shake his. He took it and lightly kissed her fingers.

"No worries, he'll turn up. Or he won't." He smiled at her, still holding her hand.

"So, see you tomorrow night then."

"Of course. Looking forward to it." She smiled and turned to join the throng of passengers as they jostled with each other to disembark. Goodbook stood still, scrutinising the crowd, looking for Door. After a few minutes he was the only remaining passenger, so he headed down the gangway and stood on the esplanade, catching sight of Charmaine getting into the rear of a large BMW. He jumped when tapped on the shoulder and spun around to find Door. "Where the fuck have you been?" he said, angry now, "I thought you'd fallen over the fucking side or something."

"Sorry Jules," he said, continually turning his head as if looking for something, or someone. "I saw Casapinta on the boat, so I had to hide."

"Casapinta?"

"Yes, you know, the surveillance snoop that caught me at the Oceanic."

"Wow. You sure?"

"Positive" said Door, still looking around the waterfront, "let's get away from here."

Goodbook nodded and tapped his nose with his finger and turned abruptly away from Door, crossing the road and passing through the outside areas of a number of restaurants, whose tables and chairs overflowed onto the pavement.

He headed south-east along Tigne seafront. Door stayed on the waterfront side, where there were far fewer people, and followed Goodbook. After a few hundred paces Goodbook crossed the road to re-join Door on the waterfront. It was much quieter here away from the shops and restaurants and they were alone. Goodbook lit two cheroots and gave one to Door.

They stood quietly for a while, Goodbook a little warm and uncomfortable in the glare of the afternoon sun and Door still nervous, watchfully observing any pedestrians that approached them and passed by.

"Jules this could change our plans. Casapinta has to be here for the casino opening, too much of a coincidence." He puffed on the cheroot, waving the smoke away with a shaky hand. "We may have to skip opening night or give it all away. I can't even wear a disguise, what with the passport entry rule."

Goodbook put his arm around Door. "Mate, it's okay. Look, it's gonna be the opening, there will be all these young kids on reception, all new to the job and nervous, it will be mobbed out. People queuing up, getting impatient, the kids will be flustered, a cursory look at passports is all, it's more of a proof of age thing than an identity check. Just stick on a moustache and you'll be right," he said, slapping Door so hard on the back it knocked the cheroot from his mouth.

"Jesus Jules," said Door, picking up the cheroot. They stood quietly facing each other for a while. Door spoke first, "Yeah, I guess you're right. Sorry but I got real spooked seeing Casapinta. Hid in the toilet, didn't want to be seen or worse for us to be seen together."

Goodbook smiled at his friend and pointed at the Fortina Hotel across the road. "Mate, we're gonna go in there, get out of the sun, have a nice cool beer and maybe a Jack Daniels or two and just settle down. Everything will be just fine. No worries."

CHAPTER TWENTY

MALTA - RABAT - CASINO MDINA

Browning, Shruggy, Jan Van der Heyden and two slot technicians were unpacking the slot machines on the casino floor before wheeling them over to the slot machine play zone. Browning thought they looked like Pharoahs' sarcophagi, ginormous in their wooden crates. Syd Cowper approached, picking his way gingerly through the discarded cardboard, wooden slats, and lumps of polystyrene packing. He pointed to the rows of machines still waiting to be unpacked. "How's it going Doug? Gonna make it in time?"

"Well, it's going to be a close thing," said Browning, "but at least Jan Van knows what he's doing and is confident we'll get them all working in time. But I dunno, I'm just mucking-in, hoping he's right." He smiled at Cowper. "And how's the training going, still happy?" Since he had brought in Shruggy to take over from Cowper he had been concerned that he, Cowper, would be okay with it and accept the situation. Especially as Cowper had been holding the fort since Lloyd Baker left without any warning.

Cowper smiled at him, "Yes, all good. To be honest the blackjack team could be a little sharper but our roulette dealers, all trainees, are doing fine. And Shruggy's been just great, encouraging them and calming them with his 's'obvious, know what I mean' routine". Cowper shrugged, mimicking Shruggy's habit. "But they are all a bit nervous about the Fun Night".

Browning nodded. The Fun Night would be the first time the trainees would deal to persons other than their colleagues and trainers, namely their parents and friends, who would be invited along for a 'Charity Night' with play-for-fun-chips and gifts for the players who accumulated the biggest winnings at the end of the session. It was a great way to expose the trainees to live action and for them to interact with the experienced staff and management.

"Anyway," said Cowper, "there's an American bloke at reception who wants to see you. A Mr Meadows." Browning smiled. "Actually, Syd he's our boss, so can you bring him here please? Also please arrange a management security ID tag for him with access to all areas".

Cowper nodded and left the room, carefully negotiating the packaging debris which by now had completely covered the casino floor. Browning called over to Shruggy, who, needing no further invitation to stop unpacking, ambled over.

"Doug, mate, we're gonna go close with these slots. S'obvious innit. Gonna take us all day to unpack 'em and who knows how long to wire 'em all up. When's the opening night? Five days? Is that right?" He shrugged, twice, agitated. "Never mind the Fun Night coming up."

"Shruggy, just keep calm and drink beer." He smiled at his old friend. " Jan Van will fix it, or he won't. But right now, I need you to focus because Meadows is here and you need to meet him, and with your natural charm and way with words, leave him feeling comfortable that you're absolutely the right man for this job. Got it?" Shruggy shrugged. "Yeah right," he said, shrugging again, "as if he cares, takes your word for it he does. S'obvious innit?"

Browning laughed and Cowper re-appeared with Meadows in tow, the pair of them treading carefully through the packing case debris as they approached.

"Mr Meadows to see you, Doug. I'll be back with his ID," he said, scuttling away.

Meadows held out his hand to Browning. "Good to see you, Doug. I need an ID?"

"You do, and so do I," he said, pointing to the ID badge attached to his shirt. "Staff and management have to wear ID badges at all times, front of house, and we provide temporary badges for visitors outside opening hours. So, if it's okay with you, we'll get you a badge. Then surveillance and security won't bother you while you're in the facility."

"Okay, no problem for me. Does Grima have to wear one too?" he smiled at Browning with raised eyebrows.

"Yes, he does," said Browning, also with a raised eyebrow smile, "but he ain't so happy about it, him being the owner and all. Thinks he's above all that."

Browning turned to face Shruggy and bring him into the conversation.

"Philip, this is Ray Shoulders, or Shruggy as he is universally known."

"Pleased to meet you sir," said Shruggy, offering his hand. Meadows shook it.

"Heard a lot about you Shruggy, Douglas has great faith in you."

"Well, s'obvious innit, we known each other a long time, worked together here and there." He shrugged.

Meadows looked intently at him. "So, tell me Shruggy, do you think we will be open on time, all systems go?"

"Absolutely," said Shruggy, confidently returning his gaze. "But if you will excuse me Mr Meadows sir, I better get back to unpacking the slot machines."

He nodded at the two men and returned to the casino floor.

Meadows looked surprised at Shruggy's hurried departure, but Browning led him to a lounge area next to the casino bar where they sat down. At the bar itself a couple of people were busy stocking the shelves behind the counter with bottles of wine and spirits while two women cleaned the mirrored backdrop, chatting away in Maltese.

"So, tell me Philip," said Browning, waving his hand in a sweeping gesture, "what do you think of your casino? Bearing in mind it's not quite finished yet."

"Looks pretty good Doug I have to say. Pretty good. It's small of course but looks good. Got a nice feel to it."

"Yes, I like it too. Of course, Grima and his people did the decor and Lloyd Baker did the schematic for the table games and the slots. All in all, it works but once we're up and running Shruggy and I will tweak it a bit."

Meadows reached into his pocket and extracted his buzzing phone. He read a message and re-pocketed the phone. "All good Doug, I'm sure you and Shruggy will do just fine here. But I'm not sure how long I will keep you here before I recall you to the Oceanic. My relationship with Grima is not so good anymore. He is a very difficult man to deal with, here on his home turf. Not so amiable or malleable as he was when we first met. The joint-venture property deal we have is going pear-shaped. And that deal was the reason I agreed to help him with this casino venture. But it seems there are some serious planning issues, which he should have seen coming, that could make our property project seriously less profitable. In which case I will withdraw my investment, over time, from both our joint venture and this casino. And in the meantime, your capabilities and expertise are more valuable to me in Atlantic City."

They were silent for a while, as Browning considered this revelation. Finally, he spoke. "Well, I'm happy to do whatever you think is best, but if I'm going to be recalled I would like to make sure this place is really up and running and working well before I leave, especially during the time that you still have a financial interest in the operation. After that, Shruggy is more than capable of stepping up to the plate and running the place, providing both you and Grima are okay with him."

Meadows nodded but failed otherwise to respond. Browning looked intently at him but was unable to read anything into his expression. Make a good poker player this one. Time to try a different tack. "I heard from Nina that her audition didn't go so well. Didn't get the part but they liked her and put her on standby. Whatever that might be."

Now Meadows responded. "The thing about Nina is that she has a good voice, but she lacks a bit of technique which can lead to a flat note in a song sometimes. Which in turn undermines her confidence. Which can often lead to another flat note. And so on. And no amount of coaching can seem to fix it. So frankly I wasn't really surprised that she was turned down. But it was good for her confidence to go to the UK and do a high-profile audition at least, even if she wasn't cast in the show." He smiled at Browning. "But it seems to have turned out well for her, in a way, in that she hooked up with you when you were in London together."

Browning was unsure just what Meadows meant by 'hooked up with you'. Was he alluding to the fact that he knew they were lovers? Or just commenting, without judgement, on the time they had spent together. After all it was Meadows who had asked him to meet up with her in London. He decided naivety was the best policy.

"Well Philip, I've been thinking that maybe Nina could be our opening act here. For a week or two. It could be good for her, build her confidence a bit. What do you think?" Meadows smiled at him. "It's okay with me if it's okay with her, and Grima of course. I know he has the idea that some local girl he knows will open here. But if you can square it with him, it's fine. And it will look good on Nina's CV back home, a gig in Europe. Right now, she's still in London for a day or two so you need to sort it out pretty soon."

"Leave it to me," said Browning, turning on his best smile.

CHAPTER TWENTY-ONE

MALTA - VITTORIOSA YACHT MARINA

A benevolent zephyr spreading warm air across Malta from North Africa finally gave way, reluctantly, to a stronger, cooler breeze that blew down from the Steppes in Europe's far north. Heading south-west, it gathered pace over Hungary then turned due south, crossing Croatia and the Adriatic before reaching Sicily. It swirled briefly over that mountainous, enigmatic island then headed south-west again, crossing a narrow stretch of the Mediterranean Sea, and entering Valetta's Grand Harbour around four in the afternoon. In the Vittoriosa inlet the many sailing yachts and motorboats moored-up in the marina bobbed uneasily on the unexpectedly choppy waters as the cool breeze swept in.

Aboard the MV Liema Gost, a sixty-foot, twenty-six ton Sunseeker motor yacht, Door barely noticed the sea-change or the drop in temperature, sitting naked on the bed in the Master Bedroom Suite, sipping Champagne and watching Elaine Grima showering in the en-suite. She stepped out of the shower and without drying herself donned a white silk bath robe before joining him on the bed. He passed her a glass of champagne. They both raised their glasses and kissed before sipping the wine.

They sat without speaking for a while before Elaine said, "Frank, we should get going soon, it's getting late." He smiled, nodded, and took another pull at his glass. "No really," she said, "we should keep an eye on the time."

In response he reached for the bottle in the ice bucket and topped up both glasses.

"Okay Princess, whatever you say," he said, raising his glass again.

She kissed his shoulder. "Well okay, but just this drink then we should go," she said,

"but, by the way, are you doing anything tomorrow night?"

"Nothing planned. Why?"

"Well, I haven't told you about this, but my husband is the owner of the new casino in Malta. Have you heard about it? Casino Mdina. But it's actually in Rabat."

"Sure, I read about it. Your husband is the owner? Wow." He gulped the wine. "I mean I know he's rich and all, we're sitting in his yacht for starters. But a casino owner. Sure is something."

"It's no big deal," she said, "he's in partnership with some American company. And it's only small, not like Las Vegas." She kissed him on the shoulder again and held out her glass for Door to top-up. She took a sip and continued talking.

"Anyway, they're having a 'Fun Night' tomorrow, ahead of the grand opening."

"Fun night?" "Yes, it's a private event where the staff invite family and friends along and everyone has play money, not real money, and apparently it's good for the staff to have sort of a dummy run. And there are prizes and stuff, free drinks." She put her glass down and put her hands on his thighs. "Would you like to come along?"

He shook his head. "Nah, I'm not really into casinos and anyway how would you explain my being there?"

"Easy," she said, laughing, "you would go as Gina's friend."

"Who's Gina?"

"You know, the girlfriend of mine who was a little tipsy when we first met at Peppino's. When, by the way, you were asking me about how many casinos there are in Malta. So, I thought you might enjoy seeing the new casino."

"Well, it's my mate Renton who is the casino buff, not me exactly. He did say he might go along on the opening night. I expect you'll be there, dressed to the nines on your husband's arm. Eh? Chance for him to show you off."

"Not exactly," she said, with a sigh, "we won't be going, Joe thinks its bad luck."

"Bad luck. Go figure. Why does he think that?"

She sighed again. "Joe's a gambler, big time, and very superstitious. Who knows what he thinks?" She sipped the wine. "So, will you come to the Fun Night?"

He clinked his glass on hers. "Look, no offence to you, or Gina, but I think I'll pass."

He put his glass down, stood up and motioned for her to stand. She did and he deftly slipped the bathrobe off her shoulders. "Frank, Frank, there's no time," she said, squirming in his grasp.

"There's always time," he said, toppling them both onto the bed. She gave up the struggle and lay back in spread-eagle repose, eyes a-sparkle, smiling at him.

He whispered. "What's this boat called in English?"

Gasping as he entered her, smooth as silk, she murmured, "What Fun."

CHAPTER TWENTY-TWO

MALTA - ST JULIAN'S

G oodbook stood on the pavement outside the restaurant Tana Del Lupo, waiting patiently for his date to arrive. He checked his watch, she was only five minutes late, no need to worry, she will turn up. A hesitant rain loitered around the street, and he stepped back onto the restaurant's small, covered dining terrace.

A waiter appeared from nowhere and held out a bound menu. "Bonjorno Signori. You wish to dine with us, si?" Goodbook smiled at him, "Indeed. I have a reservation for two, name of Tinn." The waiter smiled. "Just a moment," he said, and disappeared into the restaurant, just as a large black BMW pulled up. Goodbook's date emerged from the rear door. The limo glided away.

"Hi Renton," said Charmaine, stepping onto the terrace, "I'm sorry I'm late."

Before he could respond she kissed him lightly on the cheek, catching him off guard.

Flustered, he half managed a peck on her cheek and motioned her inside.

The waiter re-appeared, greeting Charmaine profusely and seating them by the window. Goodbook spoke. "Well Charmaine, don't you look nice. You okay with this table?" He fidgeted with the napkin.

"Why thanks Renton," she said, smiling, "the table's just fine."

Goodbook was about to speak when the waiter turned up again, placing menus and a wine list on the table, and launching right into the specials menu. After which he left, promising to return and take their order.

Goodbook said, "I love Italian food, but I hate that Italian restaurants always seem to have TVs in the room," pointing over Charmaine's head at a TV mounted on the wall behind her. She swivelled around to look briefly and turned back to him.

"There's no sound on, so it's not going to bother me," she said. "I didn't even notice it."

"Well, that's why I was concerned about the table," he replied, "but if you're okay with it then that's fine, eh." He smiled for a moment, then spoke again, "You sure it's okay?"

"Renton, am I making you nervous or something, you seem on edge."

"Well, it's a long time since I had a date, never mind with a woman as attractive as you." He picked up a menu and sat back in his chair, trying to look relaxed. "So, I guess you're right. I am a little nervy I suppose."

He smiled, fidgeting with the napkin again.

They were quiet for a minute or two as they looked at the menus.

"Have you decided?" he asked.

"Yes, I am going to have the bruschetta ai bocconcini, followed by the spaghetti marina. And you?"

"No starter for me, just a main course. Steak I think, filleto manzo"

The waiter re-appeared right on cue to take their order. Then they all three had a quick exchange about wine and settled on a bottle of Nero d'Avola, the waiter's recommendation.

Charmaine raised her left eyebrow and tilted her head to the right in a quizzical manner. "Renton, are you married?"

He sat back in his chair and regarded her with what he hoped was a surprised look. "Well, talk about straight to the point, eh." He leaned forward and was about to speak when the waiter returned with the red wine. He fussed over them as he poured a sip for Goodbook to taste, waited for approval and then filled their glasses almost to the brim.

"Cheers," said Goodbook, raising his glass. Charmaine responded by taking a small sip of the wine and giving him a nodding smile. He put his glass down and leaned forward, elbows on the table. "I have been married, but I have been single since my wife died." Charmaine reached over and touched him on the shoulder. "Oh, I'm so sorry" she said, softly.

"Nah, it's okay, was a long time ago." He sat back again, sipping the wine. "When she went, I was in the police, in Melbourne. Detective in the breakers."

She cut in, "breakers?"

"Yeah, breaking and entering we called it back then. Nowadays its 'home invasion' or some such. But back then the breakers squad also handled bank robberies and the like." He sipped at his wine as his eyes started to fill with tears, his hand now trembling.

Charmaine reached out and steadied his hand, lowering it to the table.

"Renton, what is it?"

"I killed my wife."

She recoiled. "What?"

"I killed her and my two daughters." And now it came flooding out, unchecked, like a burst dam. "Christmas day, going to the in-laws for lunch, out till dawn with the breakers on a job in Moorabbin. Two hours sleep, up again for the kids to open their presents, running late." He paused and dabbed at his eyes with the napkin. Charmaine sat listening, eyes wide, transfixed. Behind Goodbook the waiter approached but she waved him away. Goodbook continued. "Took a shortcut in the docks, a service road that we often used in the force, didn't see the freight train till I was almost crossing the track. Who the fuck drives a train on Christmas morning?" He was struggling to keep the tears back, his voice thin. "I wrenched at the wheel to turn away, but the engine caught us, on my side, dragging us, dragging us along until we smashed into a signal pylon by the side of the track and the car disintegrated. All the passenger doors were gone and so were my girls. And my wife. Not a mark on me, just a few bruises."

The waiter returned, approaching carefully, but was warned off again by Charmaine's steely-eyed stare.

"Sorry Charmaine, don't know how or why that all came out." He sniffed, dabbing at his eyes once more with the napkin.

"It's okay, it's okay," she murmured, squeezing his hand.

He sipped his wine and took a deep breath. "So, there you have it," he said, sitting more upright in his chair. "Potted history. Cop kills his family in an accident. Hits the bottle. Goes walkabout for a year or so. Meets an old police mate who fixes him a security job in a diamond mine in Sierra Leone. Makes decent money out there. Now tours the world as a YTBP travel writer."

Charmaine sat back, "YTBP, what's that?" she said, whilst motioning the waiter to approach.

"Yet to be published," he said, a thin smile spreading over his face. He dabbed at his mustache with the overworked napkin. The tension eased and the waiter finally managed to bring Charmaine's bruschetta. He served the dish and she waved him away.

She smiled at Goodbook. "You are an amazing man Renton. In just a few sentences I saw a whole life, like in a movie, playing out before me. Such a tragic story. About your family I mean. I'm so sorry." She leaned over and kissed him on the cheek, close to his mouth.

He grabbed the napkin, tear duty again. "And what about you?" he said, "tell me your story, if you feel like."

With his now customary awkward timing, the waiter sidled up to the table. "Signora, I do 'ope you enjoy your Bruschetta is good."

Charmaine nodded but Goodbook spoke to him. "What's your name mate?"

The waiter smiled, "Norman."

"Norman?" said Goodbook. "Norman. That's not a typical Italian name, is it?"

The waiter shrugged, smiled at them both, and wandered off.

Charmaine laughed. "My you have a way with you Renton. I like it."

"Thank you, ma'am. Now your story."

"Well actually we have some things in common." She went on to tell him how she had been engaged for a long time to a policeman, coincidentally. This was in Toronto where she acquired a degree in sociology and worked for some time in the corrections service. And now she was also a writer, mostly of journals associated with her work and qualifications.

"And what brings you to Malta?" said Goodbook, his composure now fully recovered.

"Well, actually I was born here but we migrated to Canada when I was three, so I don't remember it at all. My mom and dad are both gone but my dad's sister and brother are still alive, living here in Bugibba, up the coast, and we have kept in touch. Auntie and uncle. Family ties. But in truth we have very little in common outside that. But I like Malta. Don't know that I could live here, but as they say, it's a great place to visit."

"I'll drink to that," said Goodbook, raising his glass, "to Malta."

"To Malta," she replied, and leaning right across the table, kissed him squarely on the mouth.

CHAPTER TWENTY-THREE

MALTA - CASINO MDINA - FUN NIGHT.

B rowning entered the casino table games area where all the croupiers, inspectors and pit-bosses were gathered, chattering, and laughing as they waited for his arrival. The cacophony ceasing abruptly as he walked through their ranks.

Taking off his shoes he climbed onto an American roulette table.

"Come closer everyone," he said, "don't be shy. I want to get a good look at you all in your new uniforms." He gestured with his arms in a drawing-in motion. "Come on now, gather round." Making a point of looking at everyone in the room before continuing, he beamed at them. "Well, well, don't you all just look fantastic, give yourself a round of applause," he said, clapping his hands loudly. There was a moment's pause while they looked at each other. Browning cajoled them to join in. Then they started clapping and laughing and surged closer to Browning's table. He was laughing too now but made quieting gestures with his palms raised. When the room was quiet, he continued.

"Welcome to Casino Mdina and your Fun Night. Before we open

the doors and let your friends and relatives in, I just wanted to touch base with you on a couple of things." He paused to give them his best smile and motioned to Shruggy, standing at the rear of the room, to join him. "If you need any alterations or adjustments to your uniform the seamstress will be here all day tomorrow, so just drop in. Now, the idea of tonight is for those of you who are new to casinos to put your training to the test in a friendly environment, and those of you who are experienced to help your new work mates get up to speed ahead of opening night, which is two nights away."

At this everyone started applauding and cheering which surprised Browning. He smiled and turned to assist Shruggy onto the table. More cheers. Turning back to face the gathering, he continued his address.

"So, tomorrow night will be a half shift on full pay to work on any issues or shortcomings that may surface tonight. After we finish tonight, Syd Cowper," he paused and pointed at Cowper who stood at the wheel end of the table holding a clipboard, "will hand out your rosters for the first week." He turned to Shruggy. "And now I should like to introduce my longtime friend and colleague, Ray Shoulders, who has a wealth of experience and will be working with you and Syd to make Casino Mdina the best in Malta."

The gathering responded with some applause and calls of, "Speech". Shruggy smiled and addressed them. "Yeah, terrific to be here and looking forward to getting to know you and working with you lot! S'obvious innit."

Now Browning spoke. "Ray and I have worked around the world in casinos, which is only worth noting because we started out just as you are now, weeks of training, first shift nerves. All that. And then took opportunities to work abroad, Africa, the Caribbean.

And it's no different for you guys here tonight. Learn your trade, work at your game, be a solid professional, apply yourself and after a couple of years of experience here the world is your oyster. In the meantime, remember this. If you're not having fun, you're doing it wrong." More applause and chattering.

"Okay then," said Shruggy, "let's get this show on the road." He jumped off the table and joined Syd Cowper who was already organising the staff and telling them which tables they would be dealing on.

Browning left them to it and headed for the bar where Meadows and Grima were standing, engaged in a what looked to be a heated conversation, judging by their body language. By Grima's side stood a very attractive woman.

As Browning approached them, Jan Van der Heyden came up to him and asked, "Boss, do you want to open any of the slots tonight?"

"No, it's okay Jan, we'll just open the table games tonight. How is your team coming along, everyone ready for the opening?"

Van der Heyden smiled at him. "All good boss. Only about seventy percent of the machines are working yet, but they will all be ready on time and my team is one hundred percent. No sweat, you bet."

Van der Heyden returned to the slots area and Browning approached the two men at the bar.

Meadows turned to him. "Good evening, Doug. How's it going?"

"Yeah, all good," replied Browning, "gonna open the doors in about twenty minutes."

He turned to Grima. "Hello Mr Grima," he said, "how are you this evening? Excited to see how your troops perform perhaps?"

Grima frowned at him. "Mr Browning, I don't think you have

met my wife," he said, with a half-turn to the woman next to him. She stepped forward and held out her hand, fingers outstretched, palm down. "Hello," she said, smiling at him, "I'm Elaine." Browning viewed her outstretched hand, unsure whether to kiss it or shake it. He squeezed her finger tips and blew a kiss onto them. Grima's frown deepened. "Please to meet you Elaine," said Browning, "I see these gentlemen are neglecting you, may I offer you a drink?"

She smiled and wiggled her way onto a bar stool next to Grima. Browning came around to the other side so that she was now between him and the two men.

He studied her for a moment, boy she is pretty.

He called to the girl tending bar to come over and turned back to face Elaine.

"Now what's your pleasure?"

Bacardi and Coke" she replied immediately, no hesitation.

"And I'll have a Heineken please," he said to the hovering barmaid.

He noticed Meadows and Grima move away from the bar towards the slot area, the body language still not calm or relaxed. He nodded towards them. "What's all that about Elaine, do you know?'

"Not really," she said, smiling at him and touching her hair. "Some talk about asset bases and planning issues and Mr Meadows saying he felt short changed. Joe is not the easiest person to deal with as I think Mr Meadows is just finding out."

"Oh, okay," said Browning, thinking Grima would do well to get the better of Meadows in any argument, so eloquent and compelling was the man when he was fired up. The drinks arrived and they said, "Cheers," holding the glasses at eye-level before taking a sip. Browning saw Meadows looking at him over Grima's shoulder.

Browning raised his beer and smiled. Meadows shook his head, as if bemused.

Shruggy came up to them, beaming. "Guess what?" he said to Browning.

"Whoa Ray," he replied, "let me first introduce you to Mrs Grima." He turned to her.

"Elaine, please meet my good friend, Ray Shoulders."

"Pleased to meet you Ray," she said, holding out her hand as she had done before with Browning."

"Yeah, pleased to meet you too," said Shruggy, who also seemed troubled by how to respond to the gesture. So, he squeezed her fingers with his thumb and forefinger.

He turned back to Browning. "You won't believe this Doug, but you remember we was talking about Christine Apap?" Before Browning could respond Shruggy raved on, "Well, she's working here as a cashier. Came up to me and said, 'Hello Shruggy' and then she said, 'you don't recognise me, do you? It's me, Christine'."

Browning motioned to the bar girl to come over. "Shruggy, you want a beer?'

Shruggy nodded and returned to his story, voice raised, excited. "So, I says to her, 'sorry Christine, I didn't clock you at first' and she says, 'that's okay cos I've put on a bit of weight. But I've had a couple of kids, what's your excuse'. Can you believe it, meeting up with her again after all these years?" He shook his head, as if not believing his own words.

Browning smiled at Elaine and Shruggy. "Our casino world is a small one, eh."

Meadows returned to join them at the bar, without Grima. He looked at Browning.

"I thought you didn't drink," he said.

"I didn't," said Browning, smiling.

Shruggy piped up, "Blow me, did you fall off the wagon Doug?"

"I have," he said, passing the arriving beer to Shruggy. "Cheers."

The men clinked glasses. Meadows moved closer to Browning.

"Doug is there somewhere we can talk in private please?"

"Sure, we'll go to the shift manager's office, just over there. Shruggy look after Elaine please."

Shruggy smiled, "Will do, s'obvious innit."

Browning turned to Elaine. "It's lovely to meet you. I suggest you go over to the tables and collect your 'play for fun chips' before we open the doors in a few minutes time. Shruggy will show you where."

She smiled at him, "Hope to see you again soon," she said, collecting her drink from the bar and following Shruggy.

Browning gazed after her. Wow she is really pretty.

In the office, Meadows perched himself on a corner of the desk. Browning remained standing, holding his beer. "Doug, as we talked about before, I think I'm gonna have to pull out of this operation." Browning took a pull at the beer but did not respond. Meadows continued. "Don't want to bore you with the details but suffice to say this Grima is a real prick, no business ethics, untrustworthy and I have better things to do with my time and money." His face coloured up and Browning could see the man was extremely agitated while trying to maintain a calm outward appearance.

"Okay Philip. So how do you want to handle this?"

Meadows sighed. "Well, I don't want to leave him in the lurch, but it's my resources, meaning you and the team you have brought in, never mind the funds I've injected, that's keeping him afloat in this business. But if I pull the pin right now the operation will fail, and I will probably lose all the money invested so far." He stood up and shifted his weight from side to side, looking at Browning.

Browning smiled. "Philip this operation is well structured now, in terms of the gaming management and staffing levels and ability. The facility is nice. Good location, good slots, the table layout has appeal, it's got a nice, themed bistro and a really good bar. I think it could return a positive cash flow from day one and probably make a decent profit in the first three to six months. When the novelty wears off a bit it will compete with the other casinos on its own merits."

"So, what are you proposing? That I should hang in there?" said Meadows, frowning.

"Exactly," said Browning. "You said it before, if you walk away now you may lose the money you've put in and also perhaps lose some face."

Meadows waved his hand across his face as if swatting a fly. He gave Browning a thin smile. "Go on Doug."

"Well, I'm happy to stay on here in your remit, for, say, three months and get this place performing to its maximum capability. During which time you can recoup some, or perhaps all, of your investment. Then walk away secure in the knowledge that in the world casino industry's eyes you will have saved Grima from a disaster, after he was let down at the last minute by his previous management, by using your energy, acumen and resources to fund and open a superb designer casino in Europe."

'Okay, Doug" said Meadows, with a warmer smile." You sure have a way with words. Sounds good the way you tell it. You really think it will be cash positive from day one."

"Hope so."

CHAPTER TWENTY-FOUR

MALTA - THE DUBLINER

D oor sauntered into The Dubliner, an Irish Pub on the Spinola Bay waterfront. A long bar to one side competed for space in the room with assorted bar stools, tables and chairs and some booths. Four wall-mounted televisions all screened different sports, without sound, except for the one adjacent to the front door which was very loud and surrounded by a noisy crowd of youths wearing football colours.

Passing an ornate steel spiral staircase with a sign saying 'Restaurant' with an arrow pointing up, Door saw Goodbook sitting in a booth at the far end of the room, next to the fire exit door with a couple of dark beers on the table in front of him. Door went over and sat down next to his friend, rather than opposite, so they were now both facing the room. Picking up one of the beers and clinking his glass against the other one, Door said, "Cheers. You not having a Jack tonight, Jules?"

Goodbook took a pull at his beer. "Not tonight mate. Gotta keep myself nice. Another date with that Charmaine I met."

"Well good for you Jules, it's about time you put yourself about a bit."

"Talking of putting oneself about, are you still seeing TPO?"

"Yes," said Door, "and that's why I wanted to meet up. I was with her a couple of nights ago. Turns out her old man is the one who owns the new casino."

"You're kidding," said Goodbook, jolted, spilling his beer as he put it down. "Now that's a spanner in the works."

"Well, it could be. When she first mentioned it, I thought we were sunk. But I think we can still work the opening cos she told me she won't be going along."

"Seriously. Why wouldn't she go to the opening if her old man owns the place?"

"Well, he's not going because apparently he thinks it's bad luck for him to be there on the first night."

"Yeah," replied Goodbook, "bad luck alright, for an owner. Getting tugged all night for a few bucks here and a loan there by all his Maltese mates and hangers-on."

The youths gathered by the television at the front door let out an almighty cheer, slapping each other on the backs, jumping and yelling, punching the air.

Goodbook nodded towards them. "Someone scored, I guess. Apart from you that is."

"Very droll Jules," replied Door, taking a tentative sip at his beer. "Well, anyway, Elaine said she's not going. There was a Fun Night yesterday and she went to that instead. Invited me along as a friend of one of her girlfriends. But I didn't go."

Both men sat quietly for a few moments, sipping their beers. Finally, Door spoke, "Jules, I don't care for this beer much."

"But mate, this is Guinness."

"Yeah, I know what Guinness is, my boss pronounced it 'gwine ess' when we were in Dublin, you might remember."

"Yeah, I remember you telling me. And this is it. The Irish national drink. The bloke behind the bar, he's Irish, he told me 'tis the real ting'. He says this is the only pub in Malta that flies kegs in from Dublin. This is the 'Real McCoy.'"

"Flying McCoy, eh," said Door, pulling a face, "more like flying McMuck. I don't like it."

He rose from his seat and moved towards the bar counter. "I'm gonna get something else, you want another McMuck?" Goodbook shook his head.

Another roar from the football crowd accompanied Door as he returned to the table with a glass of wine. The two men clinked glasses and said, "Cheers," raising their voices in an effort to be heard over the crowd's cacophonous chants of "Chelsea, Chelsea".

"Mate," said Goodbook, "if you're sure TPO is not going to be there tomorrow then I think we're good to go." "You think?"

"Yes Cliff. All good. And you've sorted out the false moustache?"

Door smiled. "I have. But I'm still a little nervous because I saw Casapinta. Must be here for the new casino. Too much of a coincidence otherwise."

"Mate, we've been through all that before. The moustache will cover you on a busy night. Get your hair shaved off if you're still worried."

"Okay Jules," said Door, relaxing a little, "let's not get carried away."

"Right then," said Goodbook, looking at his watch and rising from his seat. "Gotta go. I'll see you in the casino tomorrow night, usual drill. You remember where the meet-up bar is?" Door nodded.

Goodbook picked up his glass and drained the remaining beer. Turning to leave he pointed at Door. "Don't forget the moustache and your Frank Burt passport."

CHAPTER TWENTY-FIVE

CASINO MDINA

B rowning stood on the pavement outside the entrance foyer
of Casino Mdina, looking away to his right at the setting
sun which evoked thoughts of Swaziland and the truly
amazing sunsets to be seen in that far-off country. It was unusual
as he rarely reminisced about his time there, except for today.
Most likely, he considered, because Nina was due to arrive any
moment and he had finally faced up to the fact that she looked a lot
like Sandy.

He was startled from his reverie as the black BMW seemed to
appear from nowhere, and glided to a halt alongside him at the kerb.
He moved smartly to open the rear door and Nina emerged. God
but she looks good he thought. He said, "thank you Alfred," to the
driver as he reversed the limo towards the adjacent hotel entrance.

Nina embraced Browning with an affectionate hug, tilting her
head back. They kissed. "Welcome to Malta lovely," said Browning,
kissing her again.

"Why thank you sir," she said, curtsying. They smiled at each other and kissed again. "Nice automobile, I felt very special with Alfred meeting me and bringing me here in a limo."

"Yes, it's the casino's courtesy car. Look, Alfred will sort your bags out," he said, nodding towards the hotel. "So, before you go and freshen up, I thought you might like to take a quick look at the casino, maybe join me in a quickie. Drink I mean."

She gave him a sidewise look and smiled. "Sounds like a plan."

He put his arm around her and walked her into the casino entrance foyer, pointing out an archway to the left of the room. "That's the covered walkway that will take you to the hotel reception. The sign is not finished yet. By the way, have you eaten?"

"Yes, grabbed a bite at that seafood bar at Heathrow. I'm okay."

They paused as the automatic doors leading from the foyer to the main casino slid open, and they stepped through.

"Wow," said Nina. "Sure is a pretty room. Like a mini-Vegas."

To their immediate right a circular bar boasted a quirky glass counter with moody, flowing lighting under the glass. Beyond the bar the table games area stretched to the far end of the casino room. To the left of their vantage point were the slot machines, laid out in rows to the very rear of the room, alongside a cashier's station.

The eye-catching centerpiece in the room was the elevated restaurant area, dividing the slots on one side from the table games on the other, affording diners a clear view of all the action on both sides.

"So, that's Bistro Romana," said Browning, pointing to the restaurant, "the owner's pride and joy."

Above the restaurant floated a huge art-deco chandelier with interwoven wrought-iron oak leaves, interspersed with countless opaque light globes of innumerable shapes and sizes. It dominated the whole area. A highly ornamental balustrade, with an oak leaf pattern that complemented the chandelier, ran along three sides of the elevated bistro floor. At the front left corner of the bistro a raised circular dais jutted out, suspended over the casino floor, featuring clear glass panels instead of the balustrade. A Steinbeck grand piano sat in the middle of the dais.

Browning turned to Nina. "That's where you will be performing lovely. What do you think?"

"Well, it's a dramatic room alright. I kinda like it. That chandelier must have cost a fortune. What's the sound system like?"

"I don't know, but Grima, the owner, is betting the popularity of this casino on the pulling power of the bistro, so no expense was spared. The name comes from Domus Romana which is the ruins of a townhouse from Roman times, when the city was called Melite. It's just along the road from here. An iconic place for the Maltese, and a major tourist attraction. So, we have the Hotel Domus and the Bistro Romana. It will be themed so that all the bistro staff will dress in Roman costumes, and the room will have moody lighting and carefully chosen medieval background music — when there's no live act of course."

Nina put her hands on her hips and gave him a sideways smile. "What's all that got to do with the sound system?"

"Ah yes, sorry. Because Grima is so fixated on the bistro he employed a consultant from Paris to fix the lighting and the sound system. Same guy who did the sound system and lighting for the Moulin Rouge apparently. Or was it the Lido? Anyway, it should all work okay."

"Yes, it all works very well Mr Browning," said Grima, who was standing behind them. Browning turned to face him, wondering how long he had been there.

"Oh, hello Mr Grima, you startled me." He motioned towards Nina. "May I introduce Nina Meadows, Mr Joe Grima."

"Pleased to meet you Miss Meadows," said Grima, "and I would like to thank you for agreeing to headline our opening at Casino Mdina."

Nina smiled at him and held out her hand. Grima neither took it nor smiled back.

She glanced briefly at Browning then withdrew her hand. "It's a pleasure to meet you too Mr Grima, and to be appearing here."

Grima looked at Browning. "Mr Browning, for your information, Monsieur Geranton, our audio-visual advisor, is one of the best in his field and has consulted for the Lido in Paris, as well as several venues in Las Vegas."

Browning was about to respond when Philip Meadows came through the sliding doors. "Hello Philip," said Browning. Meadows smiled at them all and Nina rushed over to embrace him, kissing him on the cheek.

"Hey Nina," he said, "it's good to see you. Flight okay? Room okay. How you feeling?"

"Philip," she said, beaming. "It's all good, not been up to the room yet, just arrived. But I just love this room. Can't wait to perform here." She smiled at Grima, but he did not respond.

Browning spoke, "Nina, can I suggest you go and freshen up while I sort out a drink for these fine gentlemen. Plenty of time to rehearse and have a welcome drink later."

"Okay, Doug. You the boss." She smiled at him and turned to leave, nodding at Meadows and Grima on the way past.

As the three men turned towards the bar, Jan Van Der Heyden approached Browning, who touched Meadows on the arm. "You go ahead Philip, I'll join you in a moment."

"Boss," said Van Der Heyden, "you will be pleased to know that all the slots, bar one, are up and running. The count room is setup and ready, as are all my slot techs." To Browning's ear it sounded like 'sloddechs', being compromised by the lilt of Van Der Heyden's accent.

"Ah well, that's good to hear Jan. Thank you, well done. Which one is not working?"

"It's Grima's 'Royal Ascot" horserace game, wouldn't you know it?"

Shruggy appeared by Browning's side. "Doug, do you know where Chas is?"

"Yes. Wanted the night off. I said it was okay cos there won't be an opportunity for Chas to get any time off for a while after we open especially as the surveillance team is not fully staffed yet." He glanced over to the bar where Meadows and Grima were scowling at each other. "So, is it important to see Chas now?"

"No, I guess not," said Shruggy, "but we've only met briefly so far, and I just wanted to touch base to see if everything was okay in surveillance ahead of the opening." He shrugged.

"Okay," said Browning, "that makes sense. How about we all get together tomorrow afternoon? I'll sort it with Chas so there will be you, me, Jan here and Syd. Shruggy you let Syd know? And will you tell Grima's catering girl, the F&B manager? What's her name?"

"Louise Farrugia."

"Yes, that's her," said Browning. "We'll have an HOD meeting. All the department heads together for a last-minute check that everything is set for the opening. And I guess I should ask the hotel manager as he's lending us the security guys. What's his name?"

"George Briffa," said Shruggy.

"Ah yes," said Browning, "I will invite him to the meeting as well."

"Boss, what time would that be?" asked Van Der Heyden.

"Let's say five o'clock and I'll confirm later," said Browning, "that work for you?'

Shruggy and Van Der Heyden both nodded and they headed off together in the direction of the cash desk.

Browning turned to go to the bar when the sliding doors opened, and Nina skipped through.

"My that was quick," said Browning, kissing her on the cheek.

"Yeah, just put some lipstick on. The flowers are beautiful Doug, thank you." She kissed him, "Philip sent me a bottle of champagne. It's on ice. So, I'm hoping you will come up later and share it with me."

"Like that idea. But for now, are you going to rehearse?"

"Well, I am, but only a couple of songs, just to get a feel for the piano and be comfortable in the room for tomorrow night. I'll do a sound and light check tomorrow afternoon if that's okay." He nodded.

She walked across the room and took the steps up to the bistro, seating herself at the piano. She tossed her hair back over her shoulder and smiled at Browning.

While she rippled scales on the keyboard Browning joined Meadows and Grima at the bar, their animated conversation stopping abruptly as he arrived.

Before he could speak Nina began playing an Elton John tune and then broke into song.

The three men winced.

CHAPTER TWENTY-SIX

MDINA - L'HÔTEL DE CELLIS

The sun rose slowly into a cloudless sky over the island of Malta, flooding towns, villages, fields, and cities with its brilliant light until finally, in the northern corner of the town of Mdina, a small boutique hotel was bathed in sunlight. Curious young sunbeams found a gap in the partly closed drapes in the room where Goodbook was sleeping, their rays spreading slowly across the elaborately tiled floor and up onto the four-poster bed to shine on his face.

He woke with a start, and was, for a moment, totally disoriented, not knowing where he was. He could hear a shower running behind a door next to the other side of the bed. His head hurt and his mouth was like the bottom of a parrot's cage.

He sat up and took in the room. Limestone block walls, Queen Anne furniture, a large mirror hanging over an ornate fireplace and dark oil paintings of people in medieval clothes imbued the room with a sense of a bygone age. A tent card on the bedside table advised him that towels are changed every day and bed linen changed every three days at L'hôtel De Cellis.

Ah yes, the little hotel with a French restaurant, where he had dinner with Charmaine. Then a nightcap in her room. This room. Well, 'Suite Parisienne' actually. Several nightcaps actually. It was all coming back to him now. He rose from the bed and picked up a hotel bathrobe from a sofa, upon which were also his discarded clothes. A framed portrait of a woman wearing a tiara hung over the sofa. She frowned down at him. Good face for radio.

He went to the drapes and opened them, being momentarily blinded by the sun's brilliance as it continued its morning ascent. He opened the French windows and stepped out onto a small balcony. Shielding his eyes with his hands he stared in wonder at a breath-taking panorama of open countryside and villages. Beyond them the Mediterranean Sea stretched away forever, astonishingly blue. Wow.

Wearing a matching toweling robe, Charmaine crept up behind him and threw her arms around his waist, hugging him tightly, catching him off guard. "Geez babe, don't do that," he said, turning to face her, "I nearly jumped over the rail!"

She stood on tiptoes and kissed him. "And a very good morning to you too," she said, smiling. They stood quietly looking at each other before a very loud knock on the room's door startled them out of their reverie.

"Room service," boomed a male voice.

"Coming," yelled Charmaine, and kissed Goodbook quickly on the cheek before going to answer the door, pulling the drapes closed behind her. Goodbook remained on the balcony, soaking up the view until she returned and re-opened the drapes. He stepped back into the suite.

Charmaine pointed at a butler's trolley draped in a linen table-cloth. "I'm sorry," she said, "but I ordered breakfast last night before I went downstairs to meet you. I had no idea we were, well, you know, going to you know," she blushed.

"Take our relationship to another level," said Goodbook, with his cheekiest grin.

She grinned back at him. "Anyway, we can share. And I asked the waiter to bring another pot of coffee and a cup, with some extra toast." She moved closer to him. "Renton, I wasn't thinking we would be waking up together. I mean, I don't know what you must think of me. You know," she said, nodding at the bed, "on our first date."

"Second actually," he replied, smiling, "or third, if you count the wine in Sliema."

"Ah okay. Third date then. But it's been a very long time since I, you know," He stopped her by putting his fingers up to her mouth. "Shush, no need. Been a long time for me too. We are where we are. All good."

They kissed. "Well anyway," she said, "I'm sorry it's so early, it's just that I have a big day today and I like to be up first thing when I'm working."

"Working? I thought you were supposed to be on holiday."

"Well yes, but actually Renton I have not been totally honest with you"

The room service waiter boomed out his arrival once more, and she went to open the door. Goodbook remained next to the butler's trolley. His eye was taken by a service chit on the breakfast tray that read 'Ms Casapinta — Suite Parisienne'. Where did he know that name from?

She returned with a small tray bearing a coffee pot and cup, a rack of toast, and some mini butters and jams. She poured him some coffee. "Do you want cream and sugar?"

"No cream and just one sugar thanks. Tell me," he said, pointing at the chit, "your name, 'Casapinta', is it common in Malta?"

"Yeah, and it's a mouthful ain't it? Charmaine Casapinta. At work they just call me Chas. Why do you ask?" she said, passing him the coffee.

"Oh no reason, just that it sounds familiar to me. Like I've heard it before."

"Well, it is fairly common I suppose, but Vella is the favourite name here. Probably half the islanders are called Vella." Goodbook sipped his coffee. "Anyway Renton, to get back to what I was saying before, I'm actually doing some work for the new casino here in Mdina. Have you heard about it?"

"Yeah, I think so," he said, warily, putting extra sugar into his coffee, "isn't it in the Hotel Domus, across the way from here? He stirred his coffee absently, rocked by the revelation that she was involved with the new casino. It probably explained the black limo he had seen her in a couple of times. Not a taxi that one.

"Yes, that's it," she said, "Casino Mdina. I'm doing some staff training there. But typically, I keep a low profile and don't usually let on what my line of work is. It's the grand opening tonight so it's gonna be a busy day."

"So, if you're working for them why are you staying here, and not there?"

"Because in surveillance we don't mix with the staff or line management. So, whenever I'm off duty I always stay away from the place."

Surveillance! The penny dropped. The spoon dropped. His hand trembled. Door's words screamed in his head, "Casapinta, the snoop that caught me at the Oceanic." A nervous tic irritated his left eye. He realised she was still talking. "...keep apart from them. No interaction at all. And we only have contact with the senior managers."

She put her plate down and moved closer to Goodbook, who took an involuntary step backwards.

"Renton, are you alright, you're very pale? You look like you've seen a ghost."

CHAPTER TWENTY-SEVEN

CASINO MDINA - OPENING NIGHT

7:00pm

Browning and Meadows sat opposite each other on the most prominent table in the Bistro Romana, looking on as the first-night patrons came through the sliding doors, most of them stopping next to the bar to look around and have their first glimpse of Malta's newest casino.

A young woman in a white toga style dress came up to their table. The toga had a coarse rope sash around the waist and was fastened by a silver clip on her left shoulder, leaving her right shoulder bare.

"Hi Mr Browning, Mr Meadows. I'm Anna," she said, pointing to a silver name tag attached to the toga, "and I am your waitress this evening." She leaned forward and placed two menus on the table, the weight of the name tag pulling the fabric away from her body, exposing much of her right breast. "I'll be back in a minute or two to take your orders," she said and glided away.

"My oh my," said Meadows, gazing after her. "That sure is a short dress."

Browning picked up the menus. "It is, and I thought we were going to see more than we bargained for when she leaned over," he said, passing a menu to Meadows. "It seems that Grima particularly wanted the girls' outfits to be skimpy, in the style of ancient Rome."

Meadows smiled. "Well, he succeeded in skimpy, but I don't know about Romanesque."

Nina appeared by their side and both men stood up to greet her.

"Sit down, sit down," she said, herself sitting down between them. She wore a sparkly green dress that showed off her figure. Browning thought she looked like a million dollars. She took each man by the hand. "I have some exciting news. You know the audition I had for that show in London?" They both nodded. She continued "Well they called me and offered me the part. Can you believe it?"

"Well, that's great news, this calls for a celebration," said Meadows, waving across the bistro for Anna to come to the table.

Browning leaned over and kissed Nina on the cheek. "Great news indeed lovely," he said, smiling at her, "but I thought they turned you down."

Anna came to the table and Meadows ordered champagne.

Nina was almost bouncing in her chair with excitement. "Well at the audition they didn't offer me the part, yet they put me on standby. And the leading lady they chose walked out in rehearsals and her understudy was offered a part in a movie. So, the part is mine if I want it, and of course, I do," she giggled.

"Of course, you do," said Meadows, and now he kissed her on the cheek.

"But when do they want you?" said Browning, his smile fading.

"Next week or the week after at the latest," she giggled some more. "The show opens soon, so of course I'm needed for costume fitting and rehearsals."

The two men looked at each other. "Doug, if Nina leaves before her two-week stint here is over you will need to sort this out with Grima," said Meadows.

"I'll sort it," said Browning, "and speak of the devil, he's here now."

All three of them stood as Grima and his wife, immaculately dressed in Boss and Chanel respectively, entered the bistro.

Browning introduced Elaine to Nina and said, "Mr Grima, I didn't think you were coming tonight, and the bistro is fully booked, but won't you join us please?" he said, waving his arm across the table.

"Thank you. It was a last-minute change of heart," said Grima.

"Please sit," said Meadows to Elaine, drawing his chair back and offering it to her, "and I'll get another chair."

Nina tugged his arm. "No need Philip, I have to freshen up before I go on stage."

"But what about your drink to celebrate?"

"I'll join you for that after my first set, if that's okay?"

"Sure," he said, and kissed her once more on the cheek. "Go break a leg."

She smiled at him, addressed them all with, "Please excuse me," then was gone.

Anna arrived with the champagne in an ice bucket while another, taller waitress presented three flutes. "Ah yes," said Meadows, sitting in Nina's chair, "we need another glass please."

The two waitresses scurried away and Grima pointed to the champagne.

"What's the celebration?" he said. Browning and Meadows exchanged a furtive look.

"It's to celebrate the opening of the new casino," said Browning, thinking this was probably not the moment to tell Grima that Nina was leaving.

"Well, I'll drink to that," said Elaine, holding up her empty flute. With perfect timing Anna brought the extra glass. Browning lifted the bottle and filled everyone's glass. "Here's cheers to Casino Mdina," he said, but only Meadows and Elaine responded with a smile and, "Cheers". Grima looked grim. Browning looked at the man. Gonna be a long night.

7:30pm

When Door arrived the casino reception area was overflowing with a noisy crowd of people jostling for position to gain entry. After several minutes he managed to edge himself to the front of the throng and present his passport to the girl on the desk. She photocopied it and returned it to him, failing to even look at the photo of Mr Frank Burt, sans moustache.

"Welcome to Casino Mdina," she said without looking at him, reaching for the passport of the next patron. Once inside he stopped by the bar to take stock of the layout of the casino and mentally ticked the location of the two emergency exits and the toilets, next to the cashier's cage. He went over to the table games area and walked around for a few minutes before choosing to play American roulette on table number AR2.

He stood in his preferred location at the very end of the table, the furthest point from the inspector, and bought-in for colour chips with a value of one Euro each. He was placing a few chips on each spin for a minute or two when a cocktail waitress approached him from the side.

"Would you care for a drink sir?" she said, all smiles. He turned to face her and told her he didn't, but his gaze was taken over her shoulder where he saw Elaine Grima sitting at a table in the bistro. Crap, she said she wasn't coming. He immediately signalled to the croupier to cash in his colour chips. After what seemed like an age, during which he resisted the urge to look back over his shoulder at Elaine, the croupier paid him out in cash chips.

He walked around the roulette pit to table number AR1 and took the end seat at the side of the table. So, he now had his back to the bistro and could not be spotted by Elaine. He bought in for colour chips at a value of one Euro, as before, and began to play.

8:00pm

Goodbook finally made it through the melee at reception and seated himself on a high stool at the bar. He ordered a Jack Daniels and had a good look around the room. He spotted Door almost immediately, sitting at a roulette table. Not in a mechanic's preferred position, but the hot spot, at the end of the table, was taken.

Door turned his head a little and Goodbook almost spilt his drink when he saw the fake moustache. It was huge. Never mind the moustache, Door also had mascara on his eyebrows to make them bigger and eye-liner pencil around his eyes. Way to go Cliff my boy, you look like a Mexican bandit. Viva Zapata. All that's missing is the sombrero.

He ordered another drink and wondered if Charmaine had seen

him yet. He felt a little guilty about not telling Door that she, the feared Casapinta, was in fact working with surveillance at this casino. Yet he figured that her knowing him, albeit as Renton Tinn, made him a sort of 'double decoy'. She would recognise him of course, but in context as her lover, not as part of a crew. So, he decided to run with it, and tell Door when they met up after their hit on the casino. He was sure Door would understand. Always assuming they didn't get caught of course.

8:30pm

Shruggy stood at the bottom of the steps leading up to the bistro and motioned to Browning to come down to him. Browning did, after excusing himself from the table. "What's up?" he said, to which Shruggy shrugged. "Not exactly sure. Chas wants to see you up in surveillance."

"Okay, I'm on my way. How's it all going so far?"

"Well, you know how it is, all the punters looking to play on the low-limit tables, wanting more of them. New dealers are bags of nerves. Too slow to catch a cold. Jan Van telling me how busy his slots are. Syd getting impatient with the pit bosses. Usual shit. S'obvious innit?" He shrugged.

At the door to surveillance Browning punched in the code on the entry keypad and let himself in to find Chas waiting for him by the door. "Sorry to drag you away but there's something I need to tell you, something you need to see."

Curious, Browning said, "Okay," and followed her to the central monitor desk. She pressed a button and threw a live feed onto the main monitor screen, which showed a much larger than average man sitting next to the wheel on AR1, playing every other spin or two using ten and twenty Euro cash chips. Browning noted that he had very big hands, was in good physical condition, and had his own well-groomed hair and a moustache. About fifty. Ex-cop most likely.

He looked at Chas. "And?"

"I know him," she replied, "and he's playing. So, protocol demands that I inform you."

"So, how well do you know him?"

"His name is Renton and I met him here in Malta, in Sliema. He's an Australian ex-cop and we've dated a couple of times."

Browning grinned at her. "Do you also know him, perhaps, in the biblical sense?" She blushed. He laughed. "It's cool Charmaine, good on you. And thanks for the protocol observance. Appreciate. Guess you'll be keeping an eye on him. Eh?"

She smiled and nodded, and they both turned back to look at the screen.

Browning turned to her and said, "Can you pan out a bit, pick up the guy next to your friend? He looks familiar."

"Sure." She toggled a switch and the camera zoomed out so that now both men were on the screen

"Yeah. I think I know this guy. Zoom out so I can see all the players."

The image panned out and Browning looked intently at each of the players on AR1.

"There," he said, tapping the screen. "The tall guy on the end. I recognise him. He's a mechanic and the guy sitting next to your Renton is the decoy." He tapped the screen again. "This one, looks like a teenager. We christened him 'Baby Face' at the Oceanic. This is the crew that got away from us, you know, when I disarmed that loser Breton."

"Punched his lights out more like," said Chas, "and now they've turned up here in Malta. Small world in casinos ain't it?"

Browning turned towards the door. "Call Shruggy in the blackjack pit and tell him to get a uniformed security man and head towards AR1 and pick up Baby Face, but to wait until I get there."

Back on AR1 Goodbook was playing 'small, small' as he called it, betting even money chances with a random bet on a number every other spin or two. He was waiting for the sign from Door that he was going to start the run. Then he saw the man standing next to Door drop a slug on the winning number. What are the odds? A mechanic. Another crew on this table. Did Door see the top hat? Door's face gave nothing away. Goodbook looked at the other players for a sign that anyone else might have seen it.

The table inspector called, "Late bet," and the female croupier duly removed the colour chip placed on the winning number by the mechanic, who held his palms up in an apologetic gesture, smiling at the croupier. When she came to make the payouts, the guy next to Goodbook, a small man who looked too young even to be in a casino, claimed the cash chip payout. The decoy. Yessir. Goodbook considered all this information in a nano-second and decided it was too risky to continue. If he'd made the sloppy mechanic, then surveillance would certainly make him too. Casapinta would spot him in a heartbeat. So, he activated the code. Exactly as he had done in Tallin, he picked up his cash chips and stood up to move away from the table, knocking his stool into the decoy sitting next to him. "Strewth," he said, in his unmistakeable Aussie drawl, "sorry mate," and headed off towards the cash desk.

Door reacted immediately, stacking up his colour chips and putting the cash chips in his pocket. He signed to the inspector to watch his chips. "Need the loo," he said, and the inspector nodded. He walked slowly across the floor in the direction of the toilets, but his target area was reception. He continued walking but looked back over his shoulder to see a uniformed security guard approaching AR1, and he collided with Elaine Grima. Instinctively he grabbed her arm to prevent her from falling.

"Oh, sorry miss," he said, and then realised who she was. And she recognised him. "Is that you Frank? It is, isn't it? My god, look at you, what's with the moustache and the eye make up?" she said, trying to regain her composure, smoothing down her dress.

He gave her his best rueful grin, "Wearing it for a bet, you know, for charity."

Meanwhile, Browning closed in on AR1 and stood behind the mechanic at the end of the table. Shruggy and the uniformed security guard arrived and when Browning pointed at Baby Face, they stood behind him. Browning tapped the mechanic on the shoulder. "Excuse me sir, I'm the casino manager and I would like you to stop playing and come with me to the office please."

The man turned to face Browning and said, "Now why would I want to do that?" with a slight accent that Browning placed as East European. A flashback, Breton had responded like that, almost word for word, when confronted at the Oceanic.

"I think you know why sir. So please collect your cash chips and come with me. We will sort out your colour chips for you, I don't think we need a scene, do we?"

The mechanic turned back to the table to pick up his cash chips and nodded at the decoy who abruptly stood up and turned to leave the table, only to be confronted by Shruggy and the security guard. The mechanic shrugged his shoulders and said to Browning, "Okay, let's go."

Browning stayed close alongside the mechanic as they walked away from the table, two or three yards in front of Shruggy and the security guard escorting Baby Face. Abruptly, and with amazing speed, the mechanic raised his arm and lashed out with his elbow, trying to slam it into Browning's head. But the elbow bounced off his shoulder, landing only a glancing blow on his left ear. Browning took two quick steps and swung around in front of the mechanic, hammering him squarely on the jaw with a right hook. The man staggered back and crashed into the deeply conversing Door and Elaine, his flailing arms and toppling frame taking the three of them down into an ungainly scrimmage on the floor. Elaine screamed. Browning heard Nina murder a note in the background.

Behind them Baby Face kicked backwards onto the security guard's shin and made a bolt for it. Browning managed to grab the man's arm as he went past but the decoy swung round, and too late Browning saw the knife. The first slash sliced him across his cheek. Blood spurted from his face, and he saw the crazed look on the decoy's face, the blade came at him again with lighting-speed and knew he was too slow. Then from nowhere, a massive fist slammed into the side of the decoy's head with staggering force. The decoy crashed to the floor, blood oozing from his ear.

Goodbook was crouched over him, his bloodied fist poised for another strike. Seeing the man was out cold he relaxed, stood up and turned to face Browning. "Sorry to interfere mate," he said, putting his hand on Browning's shoulder, "but you maybe wanna get that scratch looked at."

10:00pm

The casino hustled and bustled, all seats taken on the table games, the noise from the slot machines guaranteeing a good level of action. The fully patronised bar had customers three-deep on all sides, every bar stool taken. The tables in the bistro were all still occupied with a mix of diners and after-dinner drinkers. It seemed to Grima that the upper crust of the Maltese elite had turned out in their droves, curious to see the new casino and to sample its wares. He smiled. From his vantage point on their table in the bistro he could take it all in. He called Anna over and ordered more champagne.

Sitting with him and Elaine at the now enlarged table were Shruggy, Charmaine, Goodbook, Meadows, Nina and Browning who was sporting a large pad of lint stuck to his face with sticking plaster. Nina was fussing over him, seeking his promise to have the wound stitched. Browning reassured her the hotel doctor was on his way.

Charmaine chided Goodbook for taking on a man with a knife. He countered by saying if he hadn't, then Browning might have had a third nostril or worse.

Grima turned to Shruggy. "I had a word with our local Police Chief," he said, "and they will hold those pricks from tonight's fracas for a couple of days so that you and Mr Browning can go along when it suits you, to make a statement. Before they charge them."

Shruggy was trying to recall if he had ever seen Grima smile before. He shrugged. "Okay, all good, we'll go tomorrow, while it's still fresh in our minds."

"Yes, a good idea," said Grima, "but tell me Mr Shoulders, what is it about these kinds of people, this 'crew'? Why did they behave with such violence? What were they thinking?" Shruggy mulled this over while keeping a watchful eye on the casino floor.

Meadows nursed a glass of champagne, watching Browning and Nina talking softly to each other, her hand repeatedly going to the dressing on his cheek. He could see their attraction to each other. In his mind he argued the pros and cons of buying a casino in London, certainly there were the makings of a good team here to run one if he did.

A very tall, slim man carrying a Gladstone bag approached the table and, nodding at Grima, went over to Browning. "Mr Browning, I am the hotel doctor. Dr Borg, at your service sir. Is there somewhere we may go for me to examine your wound please?"

Browning stood. "Why yes, we can go to the office," and pointed the way. He turned to Nina "I'll only be a few minutes," and kissed her on the forehead.

She watched him lead the doctor across the room and wondered if perhaps she should cancel going to London and stay here with Doug. She turned to face Meadows with the idea of mentioning it to him, but he was staring at the awesome chandelier, seemingly lost in thought.

Elaine stood up and told Grima she needed the loo, but instead she headed straight to the reception area, looking for Frank, but he was nowhere to be seen. She went out into the street, but it was deserted. He was gone. Why the fuck did Frank have a false moustache? Charity my arse. She stood there, disconsolate, down in the mouth. It started to rain.

Back inside at Grima's table Charmaine took a glass of champagne from Anna's tray and offered it to Goodbook. "Ah thanks darl," he said, taking a big gulp and wiping his moustache with the back of his hand. "Just the ticket."

She looked intently at him. "Renton, given that you can write your book just about anywhere, how would you feel about coming to Atlantic City for a while. Spend some time together. I'll only be here for a week or so."

He gave her his biggest smile. "Atlantic City, under the board-walk and all that. I've never been there. Could be fun." He took another pull at the champagne. "Do you think we could catch up tomorrow and have a chat about it then? I think I've had enough excitement and wanna call it a day, if you don't mind."

She smiled back. "Sure, of course. I have to go back to work now anyway, tomorrow will be fine. But think about it please Renton." Goodbook stood, nodding at her and kissing her cheek, before bidding farewell to everyone.

Browning returned to the table sporting a large dressing on his face, much to Shruggy's amusement. Couldn't you get a bigger plas-ter?" he said, grinning at his friend. "You could land a helicopter on it." He laughed out loud.

"All right, all right," said Browning, "enough said. The doctor put some clips on the wound to hold it and suggested I get it stitched at the hospital tomorrow, stop it scarring too much." He picked up his glass and smiled at the group. "Cheers everyone, congratulations on the successful opening of a terrific casino in the Silent City."

CHAPTER TWENTY-EIGHT

THE CENTURION TAVERN - RABAT.

Goodbook left the casino and bustled his way along towards the centre of Rabat, cursing the rain, looking for St Paul's Street and the Centurion Tavern. He found it easily enough, having been there a couple of days before with Door when they chose it as their rendezvous to meet up after hitting the casino.

A large wooden sign bearing an life-sized image of a Roman Centurion, complete with sword, shield and red plumed helmet swung uneasily above the door, it's hinged frame squeaking as it swung in the wind in the gathering storm. The swirling rain suddenly became a deluge and Goodbook made a dash for the door.

Once inside he took a moment, as usual, to look around and take in the scene. He saw Door immediately, sitting at a table next to an emergency exit. Good Boy. Door was chatting to two women sitting at the next table, no surprise there. When he saw Goodbook he waved him over to join him.

"Jules, so glad you could make it," he said, standing to embrace his friend. Holding Goodbook's arm he turned them both to face the two women. "May I introduce you? This is Doris, from England, and her friend Betty, who is from Wales. Girls, this is my friend Jules."

Goodbook smiled at the same old routine from Door, but he had to admit these were top looking Sheilas, late thirties or so. "Pleased to meet you ladies," he said, with his biggest smile. Betty and Doris smiled back. He turned Door away and they both sat down at Door's table. Goodbook waved at a waitress.

Door spoke first. "So what happened after I left, after the casino guy dropped the mechanic? Who, by the way, spilled his blood all over my shirt," he said, pointing disdainfully at a couple of small bloodstains on his sleeve.

The waitress arrived and Goodbook ordered a Heineken and a Jack Daniels for himself and another Heineken for Door. Then he told Door what happened.

"Well, the other drongo, the decoy, slashed the casino guy with a knife and then I took him out. The decoy that is. Then I was the flavour of the month. Invited to sit at the top table with the owner, and his wife, who is, by the way, extremely pretty. But this of course you know."

Door nodded. "I do," he said.

"So then your mate Charmaine Casapinta, about whom you were right, she is working at the casino, and with whom I have been in a romantic dalliance, asked me to go and visit her in Atlantic City."

"I knew it. Had to be. And will you?"

"Well that all depends"

"On what?

"On whether you're up for continuing our European escapade or not, Cliff my boy. Given that we have probably lucked out here in

Malta. Too well known now. So we would need to move on, like soon."

The two women on the next table stood up and the Welsh one, Betty, leaned over to Door and said, in her sing-song accent "Listen boyo, just up the road there's a place called Roman's Den and they play really good disco music. So, if you fancy it why don't you come along and join us for a bit?" Without waiting for a reply, she turned and hurried off to join her friend who was already at the exit.

Door smiled at Goodbook. "Shame we have to leave here, it's a fun place. And of course, to use Betty's words, I do fancy it, happy to join them for a bit."

"Of course, you do. What else is new," said Goodbook, shaking his head.

The waitress returned with their drinks, and they held their glasses up to each other and said, "Cheers."

Goodbook drank his Bourbon in one gulp and took a pull at the beer. He leaned closer to Door. "So what's it to be mate. You and me still on the lam with our European odyssey, cos I'm up for it. Or have you had enough?"

Door smiled. "So far as I'm concerned, it's only just begun Jules. Count me in. Just tell me where we're off to next."

Goodbook beamed at him and pulled a map out of his pocket. He folded it into a small square and pointed to the name of a city in the middle.

"Tashkent," he declared, beaming.

"Tashkent," said Door. "Where the fuck is that?"

Goodbook smiled. "Uzbekistan."

THE END

www.ingramcontent.com/pod-product-compliance
Lightning Source LLC
Chambersburg PA
CBHW030545030726
47495CB00004B/1135

*9 7 8 1 8 7 6 4 9 8 9 4 8 *